ISLAND OF FLOWERS

'Swallowfield' had belonged to Bethany Tyler's family for generations, but now Aunt Sophie, who lived on Jersey, was claiming her share of the property. It seemed that the only way of raising the capital was to sell the house, but then, unexpectedly, Justin Rochel arrived in Sussex and things took on a new dimension. Bethany accompanied her father and sister to Jersey, where there were shocks in store for her. She was attracted to Justin, but could she trust him?

Books by Jean M. Long
Published by The House of Ulverscroft:

THE MAN WITH GRANITE EYES
CORNISH RHAPSODY
TO DREAM OF GOLD APPLES
ISLAND SERENADE
MUSIC OF THE HEART
BENEATH A LAKELAND MOON

JEAN M. LONG

◆

ISLAND OF FLOWERS

Complete and Unabridged

ULVERSCROFT
Leicester

First published in Great Britain in 1999

First Large Print Edition
published 1999

British Library CIP Data

Long, Jean M.
    Island of flowers.—Large print ed.—
Ulverscroft large print series: romance
1. Love stories
2. Large type books
I. Title
823.9′14 [F]

ISBN 0–7089–4026–9

Published by
F. A. Thorpe (Publishing) Ltd.
Anstey, Leicestershire
Set by Words & Graphics Ltd.
Anstey, Leicestershire
Printed and bound in Great Britain by
T. J. International Ltd., Padstow, Cornwall

This book is printed on acid-free paper

For my neighbour, Trixie

1

The bookshop doorbell clanged fiercely. Bethany, intent on examining a set of leather-bound books, did not look up immediately. When she did so it was to find herself being surveyed by a pair of dark brown eyes. The man leaning casually against the counter was probably in his mid-thirties and of medium build with a thatch of near-black hair.

'Good afternoon. What can I do for you?'

The question was left unanswered, however, for just then a series of thuds and a simultaneous cry of alarm came from somewhere at the back of the shop. With one accord the stranger and Bethany rushed into the small stock-room.

'Lily — whatever's happened?' Bethany, her grey eyes full of concern, knelt beside her elderly assistant who lay sprawled on the floor surrounded by piles of books.

'I'm all right — there's no harm done,' she assured them breathlessly. 'I was just trying to reach them books when they fell on top of me and I lost my footing.'

The stranger helped her to her feet, established that there really were no bones

1

broken and sat her comfortably on a chair.

'Make her a cup of tea whilst I mind the shop,' he told Bethany, in a voice that brooked no argument.

Surprised, Bethany obeyed him. When she returned, a few moments later, she found Lily chatting away, nineteen to the dozen, with their would-be customer. Amused, Bethany offered him a mug of tea, but he declined.

'Thank you for your help. By the way, you never did say what it was you wanted . . . '

He smiled. 'Never mind, it'll keep. I'll call again tomorrow. Goodbye for now.'

'Cor, he was a proper gentleman, Miss Tyler!' Lily said, as soon as the door closed behind him. 'So courteous and so good-looking.'

'You're not looking for a toy boy, are you Lily?' Bethany enquired, laughing as the older woman protested vehemently.

Shortly afterwards, Bethany closed up the bookshop and drove the four miles to Applebourne where they both lived. After dropping Lily off at her cottage, she continued through the village. Rounding a bend, Swallowfield came suddenly into view. It was an imposing red brick house built in the early part of the century and set in about an acre of ground.

The 'phone was ringing as she entered the

2

hall. She snatched it up to hear her father's deep resonant tones coming down the line. By the time she had finished speaking with him she felt completely bemused and barely had time to collect her thoughts together before her young sister arrived home from school.

'This has got to be one of the worst days of my life!' Amber announced and threw herself moodily onto the sofa looking every inch the Drama Queen.

Having listened to her stream of complaints, Bethany said, 'Amber I'm sorry you don't like your new school and that you don't seem to be making any friends but — well, perhaps things would get better if you persevered.'

Amber tossed back her blonde curls petulantly, her pretty face spoilt by a scowl. 'They certainly can't get any worse . . . Still, at least I've got Swallowfield to come home to . . . ' She trailed off as she saw the grave expression on her sister's face. 'Beth, what's wrong?'

Bethany crossed to the window and stood gazing out onto the expanse of velvet lawns and beautifully tended herbaceous borders glowing with jewel-like colours, beyond which stretched a hedge of dark green conifers. There was a dull ache in her throat as she turned to her sister.

3

'Amber — you must try to understand what I'm going to tell you,' she said in a rush. 'I'm sorry, love, there's no easy way to say this. I've just been speaking to Daddy in Jersey and he's — he's told me . . . Oh, Amber, I'm afraid we're going to have to sell Swallowfield because Aunt Sophie needs her capital and . . . '

Amber flung herself at her. 'Whatever are you talking about, Beth? It's a mistake! Daddy would never sell Swallowfield. Never!'

Bethany put an arm round her sister's shoulders. 'Darling, I realise this has come as a terrible shock, but you must listen to me. Daddy's done everything in his power to try to prevent this from happening, but I'm afraid it's not that simple. You see there are things we haven't told you because we thought you had quite enough to cope with as it was — what with getting used to your new school and . . . '

'That's nothing in comparison to this!' Amber looked as if she had been poleaxed. 'Bethany, you must have got it wrong. Daddy wouldn't sell Swallowfield. I know he wouldn't. No, I simply don't believe it!'

Bethany sighed. This was proving even more difficult than she had anticipated. 'Look, I tell you what — supper's just about ready. Let's go and eat and then we can talk some more.'

Reluctantly, Amber followed her out of the room looking an abject picture of misery. The old fashioned kitchen with its antiquated range and red quarry tiles exuded an air of comfort. Bethany was fully aware of how her sister must be feeling, for the news that their father intended to sell the house had come as a dreadful shock to her, too. Swallowfield had been in the family for several generations and she could not imagine living anywhere else.

They ate in silence for a time and then Amber said, 'I suppose this has got something to do with Cedric's death, hasn't it? But I still can't believe that Aunt Sophie would want to throw us out of our home. After all, she must be stinking rich already, living on Jersey.'

'You're wrong there,' Bethany told her sister. 'Actually, she doesn't appear to have any financial assets of her own, apart from Swallowfield. It would seem she's been dependant on Cedric up until now . . . Can you remember Grandma Tyler?'

Amber picked at her chicken casserole. 'Of course I can — after all, it's only about five years since she died.'

'Six, actually, and, since then, Cedric — her — well, nowadays I suppose you'd call him her partner, continued to live in their Jersey home and your Aunt Sophie kept house for him.'

Amber pushed her plate aside. 'And now he's died too and suddenly Aunt Sophie is claiming half of Swallowfield . . . Why now?'

'Aren't you going to eat your casserole?'

She shook her head. 'Sorry Beth — I seem to have lost my appetite.'

'Perhaps you'd like some lemon meringue pie?'

But Amber toyed with that too and so, in the end, Bethany cleared the table and poured them both mugs of coffee from the bubbling percolator.

'Amber, as I've said before, things are not that simple. As you know, Swallowfield partly belongs to Sophie and the only way we have of raising sufficient capital to pay her her rightful share is to sell up. Apparently, when our grandmother died the Jersey estate was left to Cedric. Sophie, I suppose, could have contested the will but, according to Dad, she never could be bothered with the financial side of things and now it's too late because it appears that the bulk of Grandma's capital has gone.'

Amber stared at her incredulously. 'You mean this Cedric character has spent it all?' She was incensed.

Bethany sighed, finding the situation difficult to believe herself. 'I honestly don't know what's happened — only that the Jersey estate has been left to Cedric's grandson and that Aunt Sophie — in language you'd understand — now has a bit of a cash flow problem, which is why she needs her share of Swallowfield as quickly as possible. Anyway, let's look on the bright side; it's true what Dad says. We rattle around like peas on a drum in this big old barn of a place, and you know how much it costs for its upkeep. We'd be much better off with somewhere smaller.'

A tear slid down Amber's cheek. 'But I'd always imagined I'd bring my children here, and my grandchildren.'

Bethany had to smile, in spite of the seriousness of the situation.

'Aren't you being just a little premature, love? After all, you don't even have a regular boyfriend yet . . . Look Amber, I know how this hurts. It isn't exactly easy for me either, but the decision has been made and so I'm afraid there's no going back on it.'

Amber blew her nose. 'So when's Daddy coming home to sort things out?'

'He's not. He's leaving it to me for the present. I've said I'll arrange to see the estate agent next week.' That would just about give her enough breathing space to get her head around the situation, she told herself grimly. 'Anyway, cheer up, it's highly unlikely that there'll be a buyer for some considerable time — what with the property market being in the state it is.'

Bethany busied herself at the sink before dropping the next bombshell. 'Dad has said we might need to auction some of the larger items of antique furniture to raise some immediate cash. After all, they'd hardly fit into the sort of house he's got in mind for us.'

Amber drained her coffee mug. 'I didn't think things could possibly get any worse. Come on — let's get it over and done with. What other shocks are you storing up for me?'

Bethany saw her sister's face, full of resentment, and felt a surge of sympathy. 'I think we've both had enough for one day, don't you? Anyway lighten up, Swallowfield will probably be snapped up and turned into bedsits and then we can rent one of them . . . More coffee?'

Amber gave her sister a stony stare. 'You're heartless, Bethany Tyler, did you know that?'

Bethany turned away, a lump in her throat, aware that she had to keep up this pretence at cheerfulness for her father's sake. He would hate to sell Swallowfield for it held so many precious memories, not just for him, but for all of them.

'I'm going out,' Amber announced as they finished the washing up.

'But I thought you had some homework to do.'

'Oh, that can wait. Right now I need some fresh air. After all, it isn't every day you're told you're about to lose your home, is it?'

Bethany removed her rubber gloves, wishing she could say something to ease the situation. 'If you hang on for a few minutes I'll come with you. I fancy a walk myself.'

Amber suddenly vented her feelings on Bethany. 'Really? I would have thought you'd have been far too busy pricing up the furniture. I wondered what that Miller's guide was doing on the table. I'm surprised you're not starting with the books!'

'Come on Amber! You know I wouldn't sell Daddy's books. He'll make room for those somehow, wherever he goes.'

Amber stood glaring at her, looking younger than her fifteen years and suddenly very vulnerable. 'And I suppose I'm not going to be consulted on what I'd like to keep? You and Daddy have obviously discussed everything already and decided my opinion doesn't count . . . Well, you needn't bother coming to the village with me because I don't want your company — thanks very much!'

'Amber!' Bethany implored and then, deciding it was best to leave her to get it out of her system, concentrated on tidying up the kitchen. There had been a number of things she would have liked to discuss with her sister, not least of them being the incident in the shop. Lily always got on well with Amber who would have been amused to hear about the rather handsome stranger keeping an eye on things whilst Bethany made the tea.

It was a fine summer's evening and Bethany, dismissing the idea of going further afield, contented herself with a stroll in the garden. It was at its best just now full of old English roses, lavender, rosemary and a variety of colourful shrubs and bright border plants creating a profusion of colour spilling over onto the paths. She sat down on a wooden seat beneath a canopy of clematis.

There were things that didn't ring true about what her father had told her. She suspected that he was still keeping things from her to prevent her from worrying. She knew very little about her relations in Jersey — only that her grandparents had separated when her father was about ten years old and that his mother had returned to her native island taking his little sister, Sophie, with her.

During the year that followed, Peter Tyler had had very little contact with his mother and sister, but then, after her husband died, Katherine had suddenly started paying visits to England once or twice a year. Sophie, however, had never once accompanied her.

Swallowfield had been left jointly to Peter Tyler and his sister Sophie by their father. Up until recently, however, Bethany and Amber had been unaware of this and so it had come as rather a shock to learn that Sophie was claiming her share, after all this time. Bethany recalled the conversation that she had had with her father that afternoon over the 'phone.

'I don't see why we can't get a mortgage,' she had argued.

'Don't think I didn't consider it, darling, but, at my age, it's not really viable and besides, although the bookshop is ticking over nicely, it's not exactly a goldmine, is it?'

'But I could take out the mortgage in my name,' she had persisted irrationally.

'Oh, come on, Beth, do you honestly think I'd let you be saddled with it? Anyway you don't make that kind of money yourself. Besides, who knows — you might get married and want a home of your own some day. No, this is by far the best arrangement for all of us in the long run, believe you me.'

'There has to be another way round it — surely, legally, Sophie can't throw us out of our home — not with Amber still being a minor.'

There was a pause at the other end of the phone and then Peter Tyler had said firmly. 'Probably not, but I want to settle things amicably and do them my way so I'm sorry, darling, but this is how it's got to be.'

Bethany knew that once her father had made his mind up he was unlikely to change it, for he could be very obstinate and that, anyway, at the end of the day, it had to be his decision.

Stooping down she picked a piece of lavender and stood gazing at it, as if seeking inspiration, and then, sighing, returned to the house.

★ ★ ★

The next morning Bethany came downstairs to find Amber in the kitchen cutting a stack of sandwiches and whistling loudly.

'You seem happy and whatever is this lot for?' she asked, relieved to find her sister in a more cheerful frame of mind.

12

Amber reached for the clingfilm. 'We're going on a picnic.'

'We are?' Surely Amber couldn't have forgotten that she worked on Saturday mornings?

'No, not you, Beth — a group from the Youth Club. I met up with a couple of them in the village yesterday evening and they asked me along.'

Bethany frowned. 'I see. I rather thought we'd agreed that, whilst Dad's away, you'd consult me before making any arrangements to go out.'

Amber's face was a picture. 'Get real Beth, whoever heard of anyone having to ask their sister's permission to go out! Anyway, there are six of us going — surely you can't object to that!'

Bethany poured herself some coffee and pulled up a stool. 'You know the rules, Amber. Dad's left me in charge whilst he's away, whether you like it or not . . . '

'I don't understand you. One minute you're telling me to make new friends and then, when I do, you try to prevent me from seeing them. You know your problem, Bethany Tyler? You don't have any fun and you don't expect anyone else to have any either — so why don't you get a life!' And, scooping up the sandwiches and a couple of apples, she flounced out of the room.

Bethany considered going after her, but then thought better of it. She supposed that, at fifteen, Amber saw everything from a different view-point. She couldn't seem to remember much about it because, when she had been that age herself, their mother's health was already failing. As Amber was only about four years old then, Bethany had had to do more than her fair share of helping out.

Elizabeth Tyler had died about a year after seeing her eldest daughter become a chartered librarian. That had been almost three years ago — a difficult three years during which Bethany had had to make several heartbreaking decisions and complicated now by the financial problems facing her father. No wonder there had been no time for any fun in her life recently.

Clearing away the breakfast things, she went upstairs to make the beds, sighing at the untidy mess Amber's room was in. Her young sister had hated leaving her expensive boarding school last term, but their father, in a final bid to keep Swallowfield, had tried desperately hard to raise the money that was needed for Sophie.

Even now, Bethany could not fully understand what had happened to make the situation so critical. She just wished her father would come home so that they could discuss things properly. In the meantime, she had to keep a sense of perspective and to prevent Amber from doing anything too foolhardy. She was a lovely girl, but was going through a rebellious stage and could be quite headstrong. Bethany smiled wryly to herself as she straightened the duvet. Apparently, her young sister had inherited that particular trait from their Jersey grandmother, together with her good looks.

Bethany collected Lily en route for the bookshop. Fortunately, apart from a few bruises, she had suffered no ill effects from her escapade of the day before, and chattered away like a magpie.

Saturdays were always busy. Tourists crowded into the market town of Horsham and many came to browse in the Tylers' secondhand bookshop. There were always a number of students looking for bargains, and elderly gentlemen searching for old volumes of dry novels they had encountered in their youth, to say nothing of collectors seeking out first editions.

Bethany had just finished serving a delighted old lady with a particularly exquisite copy of Hans Andersen's Fairy Tales, for her grand-daughter's birthday, when the shop bell rang and the stranger of the previous day reappeared. For some reason Bethany felt absurdly pleased to see him.

'Hallo again.' He bestowed a dazzling smile on Lily. 'Are you quite recovered from yesterday's accident?'

Lily beamed at him. 'Completely, Sir — that is, apart from a bit of bruising on my sit-upon, but that's only to be expected, isn't it?'

'Of course,' he agreed gravely, a twinkle in his eyes.

'So what can we do for you?' Bethany asked him curiously.

He passed a beautifully bound volume of Victor Hugo's 'Hunchback of Notre Dame' across the counter.

'I'm trying to track down a matching copy of 'Les Miserables'.'

He stood watching her as she studied the book; noting the light-brown hair drawn back in an unbecoming style, the fine bone structure and the large, long-lashed grey eyes sparkling with interest.

Bethany knew that her father had just such a copy of 'Les Miserables' in his study at Swallowfield and that he would never be persuaded to part with it, for it was a treasured gift, given him by his mother on the occasion of his twenty first birthday.

At length she shook her head. 'This is a very fine edition and I'm only sorry that I can't help you, Sir.' She was tempted to add, 'but should you wish to sell that copy, I know of a purchaser'.

He looked as though he didn't believe her. 'Oh, what a pity . . . You disappoint me, Miss Tyler.'

She frowned, wondering how on earth he knew her name. It wasn't above the shop, but then she realised that Lily must have told him.

'Are you in the book trade yourself?' she asked, making an inspired guess.

His Vandyke brown eyes again met hers. 'No, but I am in the antique business and, sometimes, things overlap.'

She realised that he had a slight accent that she couldn't quite place.

As his hand reached across the counter for the book his fingertips brushed hers accidently and she felt an odd sensation, like a tiny electric shock at their contact. Suddenly, it was as if she really noticed him for the first time. It was true what Lily had said; he was undeniably good-looking. He had rather rugged features, skin that was honey-tanned and crisp dark hair, thick and tending to curl. Just then, someone else came into the shop.

'Thanks anyway,' he said rather brusquely. 'Good-day to you both.'

'Fancy that,' Lily said wonderingly. 'In the antique business, eh? He's a bit like that Lovejoy on T.V., don't you think?'

'Hardly,' Bethany smiled, and turned her attention to her other customer. She was glad that she did not have time to analyse her emotions for the stranger had left her feeling oddly disturbed.

It was mid-afternoon by the time she arrived back at Swallowfield. Amber, all sweetness and light, was in the kitchen preparing a salad to the accompaniment of a blaring radio two.

'Hi Beth, did you have a good day?'

'Yes, thanks. There's obviously no need to ask how yours went.'

Bethany unpacked the shopping she had done on the way home. 'Oh, what a nuisance! I've forgotten to collect the eggs.'

Amber made her a cup of tea. 'Daddy phoned up just now. I had a long chat with him and now I feel much better about things.'

Bethany sipped her tea. 'That's good. Did he want anything in particular? Surely he can't have forgotten I'd be at the shop?'

'Something about some guy who's coming to take a look at the furniture — Jeremy,

Julian . . . No, that wasn't it. Anyway, it doesn't matter.'

Bethany set down her cup. 'It most certainly does, Amber. I do wish you'd get messages correct. Whyever didn't you write it down?'

'Sorry — couldn't find a pen — thought I'd remember. Anyway, there won't be too many guys from Jersey turning up on our doorstep, will there?'

Bethany stared at her. 'Amber, are you honestly telling me that Dad's sending someone all the way from Jersey just to look at a few pieces of furniture?'

Amber shrugged. 'That's what he said.'

Bethany got to her feet. 'And you can't even remember his name? Great! I'd better ring Dad.'

'You can't. He was just leaving . . . He's got to go to St. Malo on business and Aunt Sophie's going with him. He'd already tried ringing the shop, but he must have just missed you and he couldn't wait any longer. Don't worry — he sounded cool about things.'

'But who exactly is this man?'

'I don't know — someone Aunt Sophie knows, I suppose,' Amber said vaguely. 'Perhaps she wants the furniture as well as the house.'

'Don't be ridiculous, Amber! It's only worth a few grand at the most. Oh, well, never mind. It can't be helped. Look, I think I'll go up to the farm for the eggs. I could do with some fresh air.'

'Okay, I'll continue with supper. It's tuna bake — one of my specialities!'

'Your only speciality, you mean,' Bethany laughed and dodged as Amber threw the tea-towel at her.

It was a ten minute walk down a winding lane to Appleyard Farm where there was a shop selling fresh produce. Maggie Lomax looked up, her pleasant face wreathed in smiles. She brushed back a strand of wispy ginger hair from her forehead.

'Hello Beth, I was just thinking I hadn't seen much of you recently. You're looking tired . . . When's your father due home?'

'Not for a while yet. Things keep cropping up. Amber's missing him dreadfully.'

'And finding it difficult to adjust to things down here, no doubt?'

Bethany nodded. 'It's been such a wrench for her, leaving her public school and she can be a bit trying at times.'

Maggie laughed. 'Tell me about it! What teenager can't? I should know with three of my own at various awkward stages. Still, at least she knows she can come over and ride

20

whenever she likes and she must surely have more freedom now that she's back living at home.'

Bethany grinned. 'Just try telling Amber that! To listen to her you'd think we kept her chained up. I'd love a proper natter, Mags — there are things I've got to tell you.'

'And I'd love to hear them, but I'm afraid it's out of the question for a few days because we've got a paying guest.'

'Really! Oh, I am pleased for you. So business is taking off then?'

'Yes. It's a bit slow at present but, I suppose, once word gets around things will improve. Anyway, this is a very personable gentleman.' She nodded towards the black Renault. 'He's hired that to get about in. Apparently, he's got some business to attend to in the locality. He's got a healthy appetite so I've put a huge steak and kidney pie in the oven . . . We'll catch up on the gossip soon, Beth. Have you got everything?'

Beth juggled tomatoes, apples and eggs. 'Yes, thanks Mags. This'll do for now.'

On the way back down the drive she stopped to speak to the ponies, wondering what Mags would have to say when she heard the news about the Tylers selling Swallowfield. She had known the Lomaxes for over fifteen years, ever since they had taken over Appleyard Farm. During that time, Mags had always been there for her, providing a pair of ears or a helping hand whenever needed.

So far as Bethany was concerned, the biggest problem was in not knowing where they would be living. Of course, for the time being, there was always the flat above the bookshop, but where on earth would they store all the additional stock? She supposed others had faced problems like this before and that, at least, they were lucky in having alternative accommodation. She patted Donovan's head and he nuzzled her arm. Feeling in her pocket, she found him the mints which he adored. Not to be left out, Mollie, the little piebald, came trotting over.

'And whatever would we do without the pair of you?'

Until recently the ponies had belonged to Amber and Bethany but then they had been sold to the Lomaxes who still allowed the sisters to ride them whenever they wanted to.

'Oh Donovan, I don't know what we're going to do,' Bethany sighed. Donovan nuzzled her pocket for more peppermints.

'That was a heartfelt sigh, Miss Tyler,' a vaguely familiar voice said and, startled, she jumped violently, scattering the apples which rolled in all directions. The stranger from the bookshop laughed and, as they stooped to collect them, they bumped heads.

'I'm so sorry,' she gasped, pink in the face.

'It was entirely my fault . . . I made you jump. You must live near here. Let me drive you home.'

As if on cue, the heavens opened making it difficult for her to refuse for she didn't have an umbrella.

Maggie, observing them from a distance, was about to offer shelter to Bethany when she saw that her guest was taking command of the situation and smiled to herself knowingly.

During the short ride to Swallowfield, neither of them said more than a few words and then only about the unsettled state of the weather. When they arrived, Bethany thanked him profusely, expecting him to drive off. Instead, he got out and insisted on taking the eggs from her and accompanying her to the back door. Bethany, who was not in the habit of inviting strange men into the house, thanked him again. Amber, watching from the kitchen window and beside herself with curiosity, whipped open the door and, before Bethany could prevent it, he had followed her inside and was depositing the eggs on the kitchen table.

'Do introduce me, Beth. Who is this gentleman?'

Bethany, who had been wondering that herself for the past twenty four hours said, 'He's staying at Appleyard Farm for a few days and has kindly driven me home to save me a drenching.'

Amber smiled at him sweetly. 'Then the least we can do is offer you tea or coffee . . . I don't think we've got a beer and, anyway, you're driving. I'm Amber Tyler and this is my sister, Beth.'

He inclined his head and stretching out his hand said solemnly, 'Pleased to meet you Amber Tyler. Your sister I've met several times already, although we haven't been formally introduced. My name is Justin Rochel.'

Amber stared at him for a moment and then repeated the name slowly.

'Justin Rochel — that's the name I've been trying to remember. Then you're the man Daddy's sent to look at our antique furniture.'

Amber filled the kettle and Bethany said indignantly, 'Whyever didn't you say who you were from the outset, instead of pretending you didn't know me?'

'Well, I don't, do I? Anyway, I finished my business in London sooner than I expected. I wanted to make sure that your father had 'phoned you before arriving on your doorstep.'

'Very thoughtful of you, I'm sure . . . So that business with the books was just a ploy to get to speak with me?'

'I intended to use it as a means of introduction, yes, but changed my mind when I realised you hadn't the remotest idea of who I was . . . Your father sends his love, by the way, oh, and this letter so that you'll know exactly who I am.'

Bethany took the envelope from him and sat on the nearest chair. She was only dimly aware that Amber was asking him how he liked his tea, for the words of her father's letter swam in front of her eyes and she had to read it several times in order to make sure that she had understood the contents correctly.

'My father says you are Justin Rochel — Cedric's grandson, and that it's you who has inherited my grandmother's estate in Jersey!'

Justin Rochel looked startled and, seeing this, Bethany added angrily, 'You didn't think he'd mention that, did you?'

Amber looked from one to the other,

puzzled by the sudden animosity between them. 'What is it, Beth? What are you saying?'

'If I've understood the situation correctly, Amber, what I'm saying is that this — this man is the cause of us having to sell Swallowfield. He has inherited the house in Jersey from Cedric Rochel, who was left it by our grandmother. That means that Aunt Sophie no longer has a home of her own and so, of course, she needs to raise some capital . . . '

'Whoa — now just hold on a bit. You most certainly don't have all your facts straight, young woman,' Justin Rochel protested.

Bethany looked at him indignantly. 'Are you telling me that I don't know what my father is saying?'

'No, of course not, but it's not nearly so simple as you've made it sound. There are things you don't understand about the situation, because they've obviously never been explained to you . . . On the surface, I agree that it would seem that your aunt has been cheated out of her rightful inheritance but, believe you me, that is simply not true. Please will you let me, at least, attempt to explain a few things before you judge me to be the villain of the piece?'

'Mrs. Lomax eats sharp at six thirty and,

woe betide you, if you're late,' Bethany told him in a glacial tone. 'I've waited long enough for this explanation and so it won't hurt to wait a bit longer.'

Amber's eyes had rounded. She had only got the vaguest idea of what this was all about, but she had rarely seen her sister so angry. It had to be something incredibly serious. It was a pity, because she liked what she had seen of Justin Rochel. She had already decided that he was exceptionally attractive and a potential date for Bethany, who was far too serious for her own good these days.

Justin Rochel finished his tea and, filling the mug with water, left it on the draining board. He bestowed another of his dazzling smiles on Amber and then, turning to Bethany said, 'I'll call by again tomorrow afternoon to look at the furniture. Shall we say three o'clock?'

And, before she had time to reply, he was gone.

'Whow!' said Amber and then, 'Come on Beth. Let's have supper. I'm starving and, after all, there's no reason why we should let him spoil our appetite. Actually, I don't know what you're getting so steamed up about. I thought he was rather nice.'

Perhaps it was just as well that she didn't,

Bethany reflected as she laid the table. Life was complicated enough at present without worrying Amber unduly. If only she could ring her father and discuss the situation with him then, perhaps, she wouldn't feel so isolated. It was obvious that this man was to be given carte blanche to select any items of furniture he wanted and, she had a strong feeling that he wouldn't be paying for them, either. Somehow, it suddenly seemed that what was her father's property, was also Sophie's and that, in fact, it might not belong to either of them for much longer but, instead, to this stranger called Justin Rochel.

2

Normally Bethany enjoyed Sundays. For several years now she had belonged to the local team of bellringers which she thoroughly enjoyed. This particular morning, however, she was full of apprehension at the prospect of Justin Rochel's visit later that day. It came as something of a shock, therefore, to see him in church seated next to Mag's husband, George.

Bethany slipped into a pew beside Amber who turned to her and mouthed, 'It's himself!' Bethany nodded and found it difficult to keep her mind on the service.

As she left St. Cuthbert's the vicar said, 'Is your father still in Jersey?'

'No, apparently he's in St. Malo on business at the moment,' Bethany told him, aware that Justin Rochel was standing within earshot.

'I like St. Malo. I was there on holiday once,' Colin Bryce remarked. 'I suppose you're not free to join the bellringers at a wedding next Saturday?'

Bethany shook her head. 'Not unless my

father gets back before then. Sorry! The shop keeps me busy at present.'

'Yes, of course — a pity though. We could do with your expertise.' He turned to greet an elderly parishoner and Bethany realised that Justin Rochel was waiting to speak to her.

'That was a pleasant service. I didn't realise you rang the bells.'

'Why should you?' she countered. 'You don't know a thing about me.'

'Actually that's not strictly true. Your father's told me quite a lot about you and Amber already, and I had hoped we might become friends. After all, our families are inextricably linked.'

'My grandparents were never divorced,' she informed him curtly. She looked around for Amber who was speaking to some of her new friends from the youth club. 'I'm afraid you'll have to excuse me. I've got rather a number of things to attend to before this afternoon.'

'Yes, of course, don't let me detain you.' He went off to join the Lomaxes.

There was something about Justin Rochel that irritated her, Bethany decided. He was too polite; too immaculately dressed from the expensive looking mushroom-coloured jacket and cream silk shirt to the soft leather shoes that were probably Gucci. Amber caught up with her.

'I'm going to join the youth club. I've been thinking about it for a while . . . Was that Rochel fellow talking to you?'

'Yes — I've got a feeling he's going to be a nuisance. Every time I turn round he's there. Well, he needn't think I'm going to make any decisions about the furniture until I've spoken to Dad. I have to admit he makes me feel a bit uncomfortable. It's as if he knows more about us than I want him to. I feel at a bit of a disadvantage.'

Amber raised her eyebrows. 'That's not like you, Beth. He's really getting to you, isn't he! Actually, I think he's rather a hunk . . . You haven't said what you think about the youth club. It meets tonight . . . That's okay, isn't it?'

Bethany nodded. 'Well, your social life seems to be taking off at last. Just don't neglect your school work, that's all I ask. You've got your G.C.S.Es coming up next year, remember.'

Amber grimaced. 'How can I forget! It's okay, I can handle it. My marks are all right so far . . . You don't mind if I go riding this afternoon, do you?'

'I most certainly do. We've got a visitor coming and I want you to be there.'

31

'Yes, well perhaps I don't want to witness him pricing up the dining-room furniture. Supposing we sell the furniture ages before we sell the house. We could end up living in empty rooms. We'd have to have beanbags to sit on and eat Buddha fashion . . . If things got really bad, we could always go up to London and become part of Cardboard City. I think I would adapt quite well, but you're so fastidious about bathing that it could be difficult for you.'

Bethany had to laugh. 'Come on — we're not destitute yet! You really have the most vivid imagination, Amber.'

Amber grinned. 'I know — that's why I'm going to be a novelist. I'll get mountains of copy living as a dropout under the arches in London and then I'll make millions writing about it.'

'Dream on, little sister. For the present you can earn your allowance by helping me prepare the vegetables.'

She pulled a face. 'Sorry, no time. I've got a stack of homework to do, remember?'

Bethany decided not to remonstrate with her on this occasion, knowing that she needed her support that afternoon. It was a bit of a rush to get everything done in time. Normally, she could relax after Sunday lunch, catching up on the papers or watching T.V. but, today, she was to be denied even that.

She had just managed to change into a rather sombre navy-blue two piece and scrape her hair into a knot when Justin Rochel appeared precisely on the dot of three o'clock. She ushered him into the sitting-room where they sat on highbacked chairs surveying each other for a moment or two.

'Would you mind telling me what I've done to upset you, Miss Tyler?' he asked at length.

'Where would you like me to begin?' she challenged in her most frosty tone. 'Surely, you don't really need me to spell it out for you?'

'I think you'd better — I never was too good at spelling,' he said to her surprise and she decided that he was trying to make a fool out of her.

'Very well. Let's see if I've got my facts right. My father went to Jersey to see if he could reach a compromise with his sister regarding Swallowfield which she partly owns. As I understand it, her marriage ended unhappily some years ago and she then returned to live with my grandmother and Cedric, acting as their housekeeper.'

'That's not entirely accurate,' he interrupted.

'There is, in fact, an excellent daily help and a cook. Your aunt has always enjoyed cooking, herself, however, and managing the household affairs, being a social hostess etc. and this arrangement meant that she didn't have to seek outside employment. During your grandmother's last illness, there was a trained nurse to help out, as well, and that's one reason why her capital was somewhat eroded.'

'That's not how I understood it. My grandmother became an extremely wealthy woman when her parents died — so where is all that money now?' Bethany demanded, her grey eyes flashing.

Justin Rochel spread his hands expressively. 'You would need to ask your father and aunt that, but I'm afraid you're mistaken if you think Katherine left a fortune. Oh, I agree that she ought to have done, but most of the capital had been exhausted long since. I'm afraid your grandmother enjoyed an expensive lifestyle. She entertained lavishly, took cruises abroad, spent a small fortune on clothes which she bought in Paris and filled the house with costly furniture and ornaments . . . I could go on . . . '

'Even if those things were true, which I doubt, what about your grandfather's part in all this? The money can't just have evaporated overnight. Surely he must have been responsible in some way?'

'I can see that whatever I say you would dispute and I understand how you must feel. Cedric bailed your grandmother out a number of times and subsidised her income, giving her a handsome allowance when certain of her assets failed. Neither she nor your Aunt Sophie had a good understanding of financial affairs. Cedric tried to sort matters out, believe you me, but it wasn't that easy. He always gave in to your grandmother's extravagances and indulged Sophie too.'

'Well, you'd like me to believe that, wouldn't you?' she said frostily. 'And now there's precious little money left and we're to be turned out of Swallowfield which belonged to my grandfather and his family before him.'

'My dear Miss Tyler, this is getting us absolutely nowhere. I think you should get your facts straight before you start jumping to conclusions . . . '

Amber burst into the room. 'Beth, have you seen my Maths text book? It's vanished off the face of the earth and without it . . . ' She trailed off looking from one to the other. 'Oh, goodness, you do look serious. Does this mean the furniture's all fake or something?

I have to say I did wonder. After all, how could any of this stuff be worth anything? It looks as if it came out of the Ark.'

'If it had, my dear Amber, it would be priceless,' Justin Rochel informed her gravely and then he winked at her and she laughed.

Bethany retrieved the book from the top of the piano.

'Go and make some tea please, Amber. Mr. Rochel and I were just about to get down to business.'

'So we were,' he said and took out his filofax. He made copious notes as he followed her from room to room, occasionally stopping to examine a piece of furniture more closely or whipping out a tapemeasure. His rich brown eyes did not seem to miss a thing.

They arrived back in the sitting-room just as Amber came in carrying a loaded tea-tray. Bethany was feeling more composed. After all, her father would be back soon from St. Malo and she could discuss things with him. She still could not imagine what his motive had been in asking Justin Rochel to visit Swallowfield. She had already decided that once he left Applebourne, she would arrange for another valuation.

'So, have you found anything valuable?'

Amber asked, leaving Bethany to pour the tea.

'Let's wait until I've finished looking at everything, shall we?'

'You've come a long way just to look at some furniture,' Amber told him in her forthright manner.

'Oh, I was over here on business, anyway, so it was no problem. I think your father was anxious that you wouldn't be duped. After all, you're not really into the antique scene, are you?'

'I wouldn't say that!' Bethany was indignant. 'My father's always shown a keen interest. We often go to antique fairs.' She indicated the mantelpiece. 'That's where those glass vases and the mirror came from and that walnut burr occasional table over there.'

He consulted his notes. 'Actually, that's rosewood. It's very attractive, but there's a tidy bit of woodworm in the legs. Still it can be treated.'

'Ugh, how horrid!' Amber put down her scone in disgust.

They finished tea and he said appreciatively. 'Thanks, that was most enjoyable.' He got to his feet. 'Shall we take a look at the rest of the house now?'

'There isn't too much of any note upstairs — just a few Victorian pieces and a Regency table — oh, and a marble washstand,' Bethany informed him.

'I might as well have a look anyway — now that I'm here,' he said briskly.

Bethany had no intention of showing him their bedrooms, but Amber, hurrying ahead, said, 'Would you like to see my room up in the attic? You get a splendid view. I can sit up there and watch all that's going on.'

'Like a bird in a treetop? Come on then — lead the way.'

Bethany was mortified. Amber's room was bound to be full of teenage clutter — mountains of clothes scattered everywhere, unwashed mugs, papers littering the floor. To her utter amazement it was as neat as a new pin. Amber shot her a triumphant look as she ushered them inside and Bethany caught sight of a tell-tale bulge beneath the bed.

It was an attractive room but, like all attic rooms got unbearably hot in summer and rather cold in winter; still it was Amber's pad and she liked it. Justin Rochel noted the modern desk piled high with school books and the lap top computer.

'Rather out of my league,' he chuckled, 'although they might well prove to be the antiques of the future. That Victorian tallboy is worth a second glance though.' It was a cumbersome mahogany affair with drawers that invariably stuck. He stopped to look at the nursing chair too and then glanced out of the window.

'I see what you mean.' His glance took in the garden, the lane and beyond, the church and village green.

'You'd be surprised what I can see from up here,' she informed him. She stole a glance at her sister. 'I doubt if Beth will show you her room. She doesn't even let me in very often.'

As if to disprove her, Bethany said airily. 'You can have a look if you want to, although there's nothing of much interest.' And, leading him back down the stairs again, she flung open the door of her bed-sitting room. It was very neat and very plain; the only concession to comfort being the huge armchair. The rose-pink walls were covered in paintings, however. Justin Rochel looked at them with interest.

'Whilst I can't see anything of value in the antique line, these pictures are charming.' The signatures read, Elizabeth Tyler. 'Is that you?'

She shook her head. 'No — my mother.'

'Beth's short for Bethany,' Amber informed him. 'These are hers, over here. My mother taught her to paint. She tried to teach me too, but I was rather young.'

He examined Bethany's pictures, noting the delicate brush work. They were of flowers — delicate little paintings skilfully executed. 'Have you ever considered selling these?' he asked.

Bethany, slightly pink, studied her nails. 'Who would want to buy them?'

'She's being modest,' Amber told him. 'There was an exhibition in the village hall last year and she sold three.'

'That was because we were raising funds for repairs to the church roof. People were just being kind,' Bethany said.

'Now you certainly are being modest, Miss Tyler. There would be a great demand for these from tourists on Jersey, I'm sure. They are into every kind of craft imaginable. You've got definite talent there. Why don't you put some of your paintings into the bookshop for a start?'

'I should have thought that was obvious,' she told him rather tartly. 'People who come into a bookshop generally come to buy books — not paintings.'

Amber laughed and said, 'I'd better get my homework finished. I've still got half an essay to complete before this evening, as well as the Maths.'

Bethany finished the tour of the remaining

rooms. He spent rather a long time looking at the inlaid table in her father's room, but hardly gave the marble washstand a second glance.

'Well,' she said as they went into her father's book-lined study. 'So what, if anything, would you advise us to sell?'

He handed her a list. There were exactly seven items on it.

'I would be particularly interested in the dining room table and those balloon backed chairs — a set of twelve is very saleable ... At a rough guess you might raise between eight and ten thousand pounds altogether, but — on the other hand, it could be a lot less if it were a bad day at auction. I'm afraid it's not really going to help matters, is it?'

She sank onto a chair, suddenly tired of the whole business. 'So what would you suggest we do, Mr. Rochel? Amber quite fancies living under the arches for a time.'

He laughed. 'Oh come on, it's not that bad. Do you want my honest opinion?'

'Well, of course, that's why you're here, isn't it?'

'The furniture looks extremely good where it is and so I wouldn't attempt to auction it before I'd sold the house. You might be lucky enough to find a buyer who's also interested in purchasing the furniture and, besides, if you remove it there will be light patches on the wallpaper and carpets where it's been standing.'

She felt a flood of relief wash over her for she was aware that he was talking a lot of sense. 'I assume you intend to tell my father all this?'

'Of course, and a few more things besides.' He didn't enlighten her and, after a few more minutes he took his leave, calling over his shoulder.

'Don't forget what I said about the paintings, will you?'

She was left with a strange mixture of feelings. Could she have possibly misjudged Justin Rochel? After all, what did she really know about her relations in Jersey? It wasn't until after her grandfather's death that she had started seeing her grandmother, and that had usually only been once or twice a year. And, as for Cedric and Aunt Sophie, she had never met them at all. Perhaps she should give Justin Rochel the benefit of the doubt and believe what he told her about her family, at least until it could be proved otherwise.

★ ★ ★

In Monday's post, Bethany received a letter from her father enclosing the necessary authorisation needed for her to sell Swallowfield on behalf of himself and Aunt Sophie. By Wednesday afternoon she had arranged to see the family solicitor about the conveyancing and had also been in touch with an estate agent. So much had happened in such a short space of time that she felt emotionally drained.

When she arrived home she decided to go riding and walked up to Appleyard Farm. Mags was sitting on a chair outside the shop doing some sewing.

'Hallo Beth. I was going to give you a ring, but I haven't had a minute to catch up with myself. How're things?'

Bethany grimaced. 'I might as well tell you our news now, before you get to read it in the local paper . . . Swallowfield is going up for sale.'

Mag's jaw dropped. 'No, you're kidding me! Straight up? But why?'

'It's all a bit complicated, I'm afraid and even I don't understand it all but, you see, Swallowfield is owned jointly by my father and his sister in Jersey. I don't know the ins and outs of it, Mags but, apparently, Aunt Sophie needs her half share of the capital and we've no other way of raising

43

it. Anyway, don't ask me where we're going because I haven't a clue.'

Mags shook her head in disbelief. 'This is going to take some getting used to and no mistake. Surely the most obvious solution would be to mortgage the property.'

Bethany bit her lip. 'Yes, but we can't afford to do that. The bookshop isn't exactly a goldmine and Swallowfield is worth quite a bit, you know. Has — has Mr. Rochel gone home now?'

'No, he's decided to stay on for a few days longer. He finds this a good base to do business from.' She looked amused. 'Why are you so interested?'

'Oh, just idle curiosity,' Bethany told her, deciding not to mention Justin Rochel's connection with Jersey for the time being. She purchased a few things from the shop and Mags set them aside for her. Bethany went up to the field and called to Donovan. She led him back to the yard where she saddled up and mounting, rode swiftly away from the farm and along the bridle path.

It was good to be back in the saddle. She experienced a delicious feeling of freedom and her spirits rose for, whatever might happen in the future, nothing could take away the memories of afternoons like this. Soon she was high above the village looking down on fields that lay before her like a patchwork quilt — pale blue flax, ripening wheat and maize.

Presently, Bethany was surprised to hear the sound of hoofs approaching and looked round. To her amazement she saw Justin Rochel mounted on Mags' horse, Jude, riding like the wind in her direction. She felt a little annoyed that she wasn't to be allowed the peace and quiet she had longed for but, had to grudgingly admit that he looked good on horseback — broadshouldered and handsome, and he certainly rode like an expert.

'Whatever are you doing here?' she demanded rather abruptly as he drew level with her.

'I spotted you setting off and thought I'd join you. You don't mind, do you?'

She was tempted to tell him that yes, as a matter of fact she did. She wanted to be alone with her thoughts, but she bit her tongue.

'It's a lovely view up here, isn't it?'

'Almost as good as from Amber's window,' he said and, in spite of herself, she smiled.

'I thought I'd better make the most of it whilst I've got the opportunity. You might be interested to learn that Swallowfield will be going on the market in a few days time.'

'I see — that was quick work.' He reigned in beside her. 'Have you been riding long?'

'You said you saw me setting off.'

He laughed. 'No, I meant — when did you learn?'

'When I was a child. We always had ponies at Swallowfield. Donovan and Polly used to belong to us, but we sold them recently to the Lomaxes. We come up and ride them when we like, though.' She sighed. 'You see, we tried to raise as much capital as possible in an attempt to save Swallowfield from being sold. Amber left her public school last term and my father sold some of his investments, but it still wasn't sufficient. I suppose we just didn't realise Aunt Sophie would need quite so much money all in one go.'

He patted Jude who was getting restless. 'I'm sure your father will be able to explain things to you more clearly now that he's spoken to Sophie in person . . . Steady boy! I was hoping that perhaps you might come out to dinner with me one evening before I return to Jersey.' His brown eyes met her startled grey ones.

It was a long time since any man, apart from her father, had taken her out to dinner. It would have been so easy to swallow her pride and accept the invitation but, instead, she said firmly, 'I have my dinner with Amber. She may be fifteen, but I'm still not keen on leaving her alone in the evenings. Swallowfield is rather isolated.'

'We'll make it lunch then,' he said. 'I'll pick you up from the bookshop tomorrow at one o'clock. I gather there's a very pleasant hotel nearby.' And, before she could protest, he had turned Jude and was heading back towards the farm.

'He's obviously a man who's used to getting his own way,' she told Donovan crossly. 'Well, he needn't think he's going to twist me round his little finger!' Rugged good looks and eyes like burnished chestnuts weren't going to win her round. Oh, if only her father would ring so that she could tell him all that had been going on and ask his advice.

She had to acknowledge that sometimes the responsibility of running the house and the bookshop was beginning to tell on her. There had even been days recently when she found herself thinking about her one time boyfriend, Toby Burton. Perhaps she ought to have married him when he had asked her but, at that time, her mother had been terribly ill and Amber had been so young and her father beside himself with worry and it had just seemed impossible.

She had truly believed Toby would wait for her, but a year later he had announced his engagement to Dianne, another member of their set at university, and now he was married with two young children. The years had slipped away and, at twenty six, she was beginning to think she would be on the shelf for ever.

All the time she was busy she didn't really mind but, sometimes, she had a dreadful fear of being alone. Life had not turned out how she had expected it to and, nowadays, her social life seemed to be practically non existent. She looked at her watch. Time to get back to prepare supper for Amber who always seemed to be starving.

When Bethany arrived back at Swallowfield a short time later, Amber was already in the kitchen. She was devouring a thick slice of bread and jam. 'Where have you been, Beth?' she demanded, her face like thunder. 'I've had a terrible day and I needed you to be here.'

Bethany said calmly, 'Well, I'm here now. Good, you've got yourself a snack . . . is there any tea left? I've been for a ride — just give me a chance to shower and change and I'll get supper underway. So what's the problem?'

Amber waved her bread about. 'Oh, just

about everything. I didn't do too well on my last Maths assignment and there's no-one to help and our English teacher was away so we had to do this pathetic worksheet and the play rehearsal was cancelled.'

'I thought you were home early. Well Maths isn't exactly my strongest subject, as you know. Haven't you got any friends you could ask?'

She shook her head. 'Their marks weren't that wonderful either. I just can't understand that Mr. Sullivan. I wish Daddy were here — he'd know.'

Fifteen minutes later, having showered and changed, Bethany came downstairs to find Justin Rochel sitting at the big kitchen table showing Amber how to do her Maths. Amber put a finger to her lips and, with her other hand, indicated the forgotten farm produce left in Mag's shop. Bethany, amused by her sister's cheek, set about getting the supper, trying to ignore them.

Presently Justin Rochel looked up. 'Ah, Miss Tyler, we meet again. I've just been rescuing a damsel in distress.'

'Two, it would seem. Thanks for bringing the salad stuff. How I thought I was going to get supper without these I've no idea. Would you like a cup of tea?'

He smiled. 'Why not? Supper's not for half

an hour yet and teaching Maths is thirsty work.' He glanced over Amber's shoulder. 'That's right.' He reached across and scrawled on the scrap paper. 'Try that.'

Amber beamed. 'Got it! You're a genius, Mr. Rochel. You've made it look so easy.'

Bethany made a pot of tea and then turned her attention to the supper. Presently she straightened up from the oven to find Justin Rochel surveying her. She felt herself colouring, knowing that she wasn't exactly looking her best in faded jeans and a baggy T shirt that had seen better days, with her hair tied back anyhow with a bit of ribbon.

'Something smells good,' he said.

'Only pasties from our local shop, I'm afraid. Unlike Mags, I'm not very good on the homecooking front.'

He got to his feet. 'I'm sure you do very well. After all, it can't be easy managing a house of this size and working practically every day.'

'I like the bookshop,' she said simply. Somehow she felt he seemed more approachable in his casual wear. The Jersey sweater and jeans made him look rather boyish. He had a beautiful head of hair — dark and thick, curling into the nape of his neck. She pulled herself together sharply. Whatever was the matter with her? She was supposed to regard him as the enemy — the man who was the cause of all their financial problems.

'We had a letter from Dad, on Monday,' Amber informed him, as if reading her thoughts. 'He posted it in Jersey before he left for St. Malo. What's he doing there, anyway?'

Justin Rochel muttered something about business for Aunt Sophie and went to the back door.

Amber was persistent. 'But if Aunt Sophie hasn't any money, how can she have any business?'

'Amber!' Bethany cautioned, but realised her sister had a point.

'I'm afraid you'll have to ask your father all the questions that bother you. After all, it is a family affair.'

Amber was determined to get things straight. 'But I thought — well, I know we're not actually related, but — well, if we were, wouldn't we be cousins?'

He laughed. 'I haven't stopped to work it out, but it would definitely be something like that. If our grandparents had married then it might have been a very different story altogether.'

'I think we've bothered Mr. Rochel quite enough for one day,' Bethany said hastily. 'Thanks again for dropping off the produce and for helping Amber with her Maths.'

He was already opening the back door. 'My pleasure. Let me know what mark you get this time, Amber. Hopefully, it'll be an improvement on the last one . . . Thanks for the tea.'

They stood waving goodbye to him and, as they closed the door, Amber said, 'I can't imagine why you don't like him, Beth. I think he's positively fabulous.'

'Don't let him fool you, Amber,' Bethany said sharply. 'He may be all charm on the surface but, underneath, he's a wolf in sheep's clothing.'

Amber stared at her sister as if she hadn't got the remotest notion of what she meant. When you were only fifteen you could wear your heart on your sleeve, Bethany reflected as she attended to the supper, but that was before you came to realise that people weren't all they seemed to be on the surface. She attacked the potatoes viciously with a knife to see if they were done.

3

On Thursday, Bethany had a busy morning at the shop. A party from a historical society came to visit the local museum and church, and a number of them wandered in looking for old maps and stories about the town. No sooner had they gone than a couple of retired schoolteachers arrived, wanting to track down a copy of a favourite poem. After that, there were a series of 'phone calls from people wishing to sell ancient encyclopaedias or off load elderly volumes of Dickens. She snatched a quick cup of coffee with Lily, had a chat with the man who rebound cherished editions and then, somehow, it was lunchtime.

She had not expected Justin Rochel to put in an appearance. After all, people tended to say things they didn't always mean but, just in case, she had dressed in a neat black skirt and a rose pink blouse and left her jacket hanging in the tiny cloakroom. She had told Lily that there was a possibility that the stranger of a few days ago, might be calling in to discuss some further business.

The doorbell rang at one o'clock sharp

and Justin Rochel stood there framed in the doorway, looking extremely handsome in a pale grey suit that was very obviously not off-the-peg. Bethany couldn't understand why her heart quickened a pace, nor why she suddenly felt awkward at the prospect of having lunch with him.

'I believe we have a luncheon engagement, Miss Tyler,' he said. 'Hallo Lily, how are you today? No more little accidents?'

She beamed at him. 'No, Sir.'

'You'd better take an extra half hour for lunch today, Lily. I'm sure you could do with it,' Bethany told her. 'Take the spare key — just in case you're back before me.'

Lily looked surprised but grateful and, a few minutes later, Justin Rochel was steering Bethany in the direction of a nearby hotel.

'Maggie Lomax recommended this place to me. She said she and George went there on their anniversary a few weeks ago.'

Bethany wanted to protest — to tell him that it was far too expensive and that she would be quite happy with egg and chips in the cafe round the corner from the bookshop, but, somehow, she thought she ought not to argue with him. She did a quick calculation of how much was in her purse, having every intention of offering to go Dutch.

She hadn't been in the hotel he took her to for a long while — certainly not since her family's circumstances had changed and she felt a surge of pleasure at being there again for she had many happy memories associated with the place.

She declined wine with the meal and asked for mineral water instead, determined to keep a clear head. They had the set menu which seemed to cater for all tastes with its wide range of choices. Justin Rochel ordered melon with port, and salmon with watercress, new potatoes and a selection of fresh vegetables for them both.

'Tell me about yourself,' he said presently.

This surprised her, for there wasn't much he couldn't know already.

'There's not much to tell. You know my background from my father, surely? You've met my sister and you've seen where I live and work. What more could you possibly want to know?'

His Vandyke brown eyes met hers questionably and she felt as if he were capable of reading what was in her heart. She concentrated on the melon which was very juicy and would probably splash on her blouse.

'I'd like to know about you as a person, Bethany Tyler. You don't seem to be particularly happy and I just wondered why that might be.'

The colour tinged her cheeks. 'I don't know what you mean. At the moment, I suppose I am under a fair amount of pressure, but you of all people should understand why that is . . . When my father returns and some of the workload is removed from my shoulders and a few decisions have been made regarding where we're going to live when we've sold Swallowfield, then things should improve no end.'

The waitress removed their empty plates and fetched the salmon.

'I think there's more to it than that. Your father tells me you're a qualified librarian and that you used to work at a college.'

'For a short time, yes.' She fixed her gaze on his tie which was of figured lilac silk and matched his dove-grey shirt perfectly. Did he choose his own clothes, she wondered or was there some female with exemplary taste to help him?

'And you gave up your career to come home and look after your mother?'

She speared a potato. 'Anyone would have done the same . . . She was very ill. Anyway, I enjoy working in the bookshop,' she said defensively, wondering where this conversation was leading.

'When was the last time you had a holiday, Miss Tyler?'

She started at him. This was the last question she would have expected him to ask. 'Oh, I don't know. There's never time for holidays. If I get the occasional day off I consider myself lucky. Anyway, what would I do with a holiday?'

'Everyone deserves a holiday from time to time . . . Tell me, have you ever been to Jersey?'

So this was what he was driving at. 'No — I might have done had my grandmother lived a little longer perhaps, but there really doesn't seem to be a great deal of point now, does there?'

'We'll come back to that one in a minute . . . Bethany, I spoke to your father on the 'phone last night.'

She was taken aback. 'You tell me my father rang you when he hasn't even been in touch with me. Why would he do that! What's happened?' she demanded.

'Nothing, believe you me. I'd have told you if it were bad news. I phoned him — not the other way round. He'd just got back from St. Malo and says to tell you he'll be in touch shortly . . . '

'But I don't understand. There's something going on that I don't know about, isn't there?

Please will you tell me!'

'Certainly, if you'll just listen, I'll explain. I'm returning to Jersey tomorrow and I needed to discuss things with your father before speaking to you . . . I've an idea that might work out well for all of us.'

Bethany studied the small vase of wild flowers on the table, wondering what on earth he had got to tell her. It had to be important if he had already spoken with her father. She was slightly indignant that he couldn't have seen fit to consult her first. She could have told him if it sounded viable, whatever it was.

She raised her eyes and said calmly, 'You'd better tell me what it is — this idea of yours.' She was totally unprepared for his answer.

'How would you feel if I bought out Sophie's share of the house so that she could invest the capital and have some form of income? Off shore investments are quite attractive and it would mean that you could stay at Swallowfield, after all.'

So great was Bethany's surprise that she dropped her fork. He passed her another one and sat waiting for her answer. Her mind was spinning.

'Have you any idea of the market value of Swallowfield?' she asked at length.

He helped himself to more vegetables. 'Naturally. I called into the estate agents' this morning and had quite a chat with them. Your Mr. Bonner feels that, for a cash purchase, you might be prepared to drop the price.'

Her face was a picture. She took a deep breath. 'Let's get this straight — are you telling me that you are prepared to buy out Aunt Sophie's share of the house?'

He nodded. 'More or less. I think the price you're asking is a little unrealistic, however. My top offer would be £100,000 to include any furniture and fittings — antique or other — that might happen to be in the rooms I chose.'

She gaped at him. 'Now come on, Mr. Rochel. What exactly do you take me for? What possible benefit would half a house be to you? I bet the estate agent had a good laugh.'

He sipped his wine. 'He didn't, actually. And, as the house hasn't actually gone on the market yet, things should be fairly straightforward. If you agree, then your father has proposed that we get in touch with our respective solicitors as soon as possible and, hopefully, the matter can be settled swiftly and to our mutual satisfaction. Of course, I'd need to have a proper survey done, but

I don't anticipate too many problems on that score.'

'Hold it there — you're going far too fast. I have absolutely no intention of doing anything until I've had a chance to speak with my father . . . How do I know what you're telling me is true?'

He burst out laughing so that people on surrounding tables turned to look and she wished the ground would open and swallow them up.

'What kind of madman would offer you that sum of money if he didn't mean it, for goodness sake? Don't you trust anyone apart from your father, Miss Tyler?'

She felt herself getting annoyed. He was so sure of himself.

'But you obviously had no intention of purchasing Aunt Sophie's half share in Swallowfield when you first arrived in Applebourne or my father would never have asked me to put it on the market.'

Justin Rochel inclined his head. 'Admittedly I originally only came to look at the furniture but once I'd seen the village and Swallowfield.' He paused, 'And met you and Amber then I thought — why not?'

She drank her mineral water, not trusting herself to speak. Her heart was beating a wild tattoo as the significance of what he was saying sank in. 'Tell me what possible motive you could have for buying half a house? Whatever use would it be to you?'

He folded his arms. 'I see it as a future investment and there are lots of options which we can discuss at a future date. I come to England fairly regularly on business and I get heartily tired of hotels. I'd quite like a pad in the country and Swallowfield is conveniently situated. There's plenty of space so we need not get in each other's way. Peter and I have a lot in common, Amber seems to like me and, hopefully, you and I will manage to get on in a civilised fashion too, once you stop being so suspicious of me.

'Let's look at things logically. Sophie owns half a house which she doesn't want, but she does need the capital. Your father can't afford to buy her out, raise a mortgage or even pay for the upkeep of the property come to that. You have to admit that it's in need of some renovation which is why you will need to consider dropping the asking price.'

She bridled. 'And you're going to want a say in things, of course, not only in the rooms you'd want to use but in the furnishing and decorating too!'

'Let's take one step at a time, shall we? I would only want to make a few reasonable alterations. That's surely fair, Miss Tyler.

And, after all, Swallowfield may be your home but it's actually your father and Aunt whose names are on the title deeds . . . I thought you'd be pleased — not put up so much opposition.'

Bethany felt like bursting into tears and telling him to get out of her sight. Previously her father had consulted her on all sorts of matters, but now it appeared he had a new right hand man.

Justin Rochel saw the stricken expression on her face and the troubled look in her long-lashed grey eyes.

'It's a lot to get your head round. Look why don't you wait until you've had an opportunity to discuss matters with your father? I know he won't want to proceed against your wishes, but I would point out that it's probably the best offer he's going to get this side of Christmas . . . Would you like a dessert?'

She shook her head and wanted to tell him that it would probably choke her, but remembered her manners before she regretted it.

He ordered coffee and they went into the lounge and sat in the comfortable basket chairs. 'Won't it be difficult for you to raise that sort of capital?' she ventured presently, wondering just how wealthy he was and whether it had all come from her grandmother's estate on Jersey.

He crossed his legs and leant back in the chair. 'I would just need to make a few phone calls. Perhaps I ought to explain a little about myself. My parents died in a plane crash when I was fourteen. I was at boarding school for most of the year and so, as I was only a minor, our family home was sold and the money put in trust for me together with the rest of my inheritence. That's how I came to live with your grandmother and my grandfather and, of course, Sophie. I also inherited my father's antique shop which we kept on — that's how I happen to know a fair amount about antiques.'

'And now you've also inherited Cedric's estate which just happens to include my grandmother's house,' she intervened.

He nodded. 'I would agree that poor Sophie does seem to have had a rough deal of it in some ways and so I've decided to do what I can to help. This way seems an excellent solution and should keep all parties happy. I like Applebourne and Swallowfield. Admittedly I couldn't raise the capital for the entire house, but rather than let it go from a family that has owned it for several generations, I'd be prepared to buy out Sophie's share.'

It seemed to her that there had to be a catch in it somewhere — something that both her father and herself had overlooked. She realised that Justin Rochel wouldn't even be their landlord but just someone who used the house from time to time — more like a guest, in fact. The thought was strangely disturbing.

She poured more coffee and helped herself to another foil-wrapped mint and then, to her horror, looked at her watch and realised that it was almost half past two.

'I'll have to go in a minute . . . You might have offered to make us solvent, but we still can't afford to lose trade.' She reached for her purse and offered him some notes, but he caught her wrist.

'Absolutely not . . . It was my pleasure. Cheer up, things could be a lot worse, you know.'

She walked back to the bookshop completely bemused; the feel of his fingers encircling her wrist had left an odd tingling sensation. She knew that Justin Rochel held a certain magnetism for her and felt it was probably because there was an air of mystery about him. There was still so much she didn't know about the man. Suddenly she wished she could have met his grandfather, Cedric Rochel, but now it was too late.

Bethany spent the afternoon in a trance, mulling things over and really not being a great deal of use. Lily, noting the slightly flushed cheeks and the faraway look in her eyes asked if she were feeling herself.

Bethany nodded. 'Lily, how do you know if someone's being genuine or not?'

'Ah, now,' Lily said thoughtfully, 'that's a tricky one, but I suppose if they sticks to what they says and don't change their minds then — that's how you know.'

And Bethany had to be content with that reply.

Peter Tyler rang that evening. Bethany took the call in the study and shut the door before Amber could interrupt. There were things that she needed to know. They discussed Justin Rochel's proposal for almost ten minutes and then he said, 'Darling, if you're not happy with the arrangement, we needn't go ahead with it, but you do realise that then there really would be no option for us but to leave Swallowfield and, probably Applebourne, altogether?'

She swallowed hard. 'There are so many questions I want to ask — so much I'd like to know. When are you coming home, Dad?'

'Well, I suppose I could pay a fleeting visit at the beginning of next week. There are certainly a number of matters that I need to sort out, but then I'd need to get back here to discuss the finer points with Justin and your Aunt before we could finalise things . . . Look, why don't you sleep on it? I'll ring you again this time tomorrow and, by then Justin should have arrived back here. Obviously, he needs a bit of time to get the capital together, and consult his solicitor who, fortunately, is the same one as Sophie's.'

'And what do you really think, Dad?' Bethany asked. 'Would you prefer to sell up completely?'

'No darling, of course not. I never intended that in the first place. To tell you the truth, this arrangement would take an enormous weight off my mind. I don't want to let go of our home, and it would be wonderful to know that for once, there was money flowing into it. Just lately, it's seemed we've had to scrape the barrel for every repair that's needed doing. This way we could share the cost with Justin and that would mean that perhaps we could even consider updating the kitchen at last and putting in another bathroom.'

'And what happens if Mr. Rochel wants out in a few years time?' she demanded. 'We'd hardly be in a position to buy him out, any more than we are now. Won't we just be in precisely the same boat all over again?'

Peter Tyler laughed. 'That's my girl — forever being cautious. Let's face it, in a few years time, things could be totally different for us all. Let's not look into the future, but take things day by day . . . Now, how are things at the shop?'

She had just finished telling him when Amber came into the room.

'Amber's here, longing to speak to you.'

'My other favourite daughter . . . Have you told her about Justin's offer yet?'

'No, do you want me to?'

'Not for the moment. Let's leave it till I get back. We'll do it together, shall we?'

Bethany said, 'goodbye,' and handed the phone over to Amber, telling her she was going for a short walk. She stopped to cut some roses from the garden and then made her way to the churchyard.

Her mother's grave was by the side of her grandfather's and next to her brother James' who had died when he was only seven years old from a particularly malevolent virus. She laid the roses down and stood there for a few moments, wondering what her mother would have done in these circumstances.

Her mother had been the level-headed one in the marriage, full of commonsense but, after James had died she had withdrawn into herself. She had tried, in vain, to give Peter

Tyler another son, but after two miscarriages and weakening health, was told no more children. And then along came Amber, and Elizabeth Tyler had gained a new lease of life for a few more years, painting more sensitively than ever before and becoming almost like her old self again.

Bethany went to sit on a bench overlooking the village green and the churchyard cat jumped up beside her. She stroked it absently and it purred. Presently, she walked back along the lane towards Swallowfield feeling a great deal more composed and at peace than when she had set out.

On Friday evening Peter Tyler rang again, as promised, and, by then, Bethany had made a decision. If her father wanted to accept Justin Rochel's offer then she would not oppose him. He had enough problems at present and needed her support. She felt calmer about the situation now and, after all, it would have been an enormous wrench to leave Swallowfield. At least this would be a compromise and, if things didn't work out, then perhaps Justin Rochel could let his part of the house. They would, of course, need to discuss this issue.

'Wonderful!' her father said. 'I knew you'd see reason eventually. I'll tell Justin straight away and Sophie, of course, and then we can get down to business.'

'You are still coming home?' she asked anxiously, knowing that there were still countless things she needed to ask him about.

'Of course, I'll be back in time for supper on Monday evening.'

Bethany was a long time getting to sleep that night. Doubts crowded into her mind as to whether they really were making the right decision to stay on at Swallowfield. Her father trusted everyone, regarding them all as his friends, but what did they know of Justin Rochel? As she recalled his handsome, rather rugged features, the thick dark hair falling over his brow and the dancing, rich brown eyes, her heart did a funny little jump. Did he have this effect on all females, she wondered or was it just that she had been starved of the company of the opposite sex — apart from her father for rather a long time? With a start, she suddenly realised that she hadn't thought of Toby for quite some while.

Peter Tyler was as good as his word and arrived at Swallowfield just before the evening meal on Monday. After they had eaten they went into the sitting-room and he told Amber the news. Her reaction was to throw her arms around his neck.

'Isn't it great, Beth? If Mr. Rochel is coming to live with us that means he'll be able to help me with my Maths whenever I get stuck and Dad's not around.'

'Hey, wait a minute, young lady,' her father told her. 'He's not going to be here all of the time — only when he's got business to do in England, but I'm glad you liked him.'

'I thought he was fab, myself, but Beth isn't so keen. She doesn't trust him.'

Peter Tyler laughed. 'Sounds like my girls to me — Beth ever cautious and you, Amber, like myself — liking everyone on sight and, sometimes, making errors of judgment. Anyway, I think I can safely say that Justin Rochel is a very genuine character. Aunt Sophie adores him and, after all, she has quite a lot of similar traits to you, Beth, so I trust her opinion.'

Bethany was silent and he looked across at her. 'What's the matter, Beth? Still not convinced?'

'I just feel that this has all been so sudden. There are lots of things I'd like answers to — a number of points I'd like to discuss.'

Peter Tyler suddenly looked very weary and older than his fifty five years. He ran a hand through his greying hair in a characteristic gesture.

'We'll talk some more tomorrow, eh? For now, let's enjoy a quiet evening . . . Come on, I'll show you my photographs.'

And Bethany had to be content with that for the time being. She was beginning to wonder if she ought to go to Jersey to suss out the situation for herself, after all. She was aware that her father was inclined to be rather gullible. Unfortunately, in the past, he had been sadly taken in by someone whom he had considered to be a friend and had been cheated out of a substantial sum of money, but she had no intention of reminding him of that.

At breakfast the following morning, Amber said, 'I suppose from now on, Mr. Rochel will be staying here. If we'd known we could have put him up this time.'

'Hardly,' her father objected. 'I wouldn't foist a stranger on you. Anyway, I can assure you that I didn't know he was going to offer to put up the money for Sophie's share of the house. I genuinely thought he was just coming to look over the furniture.'

'So he really is in the antique business then?'

'Justin has irons in a number of fires, Amber. Amongst other things he's a chartered accountant. Anyway, he was obviously so smitten with Applebourne that he's decided

71

to make it his base — very providential, I'd say. Good old Mags and George must have made his stay very welcoming.'

'He rides,' Amber said. 'He went riding with Bethany, didn't he?'

Bethany coloured. 'Not exactly. He happened to meet up with me when I was out on Donovan, that's all.' She began to collect up the breakfast things wondering what changes Justin Rochel would bring to their lives.

Presently, Peter Tyler 'phoned Lily and told her to take the morning off and then they set out for the bookshop dropping Amber off at school en route.

'So what are all these questions you've been storing up for me?' he asked Bethany as they headed towards the town centre.

'Well, for a start, what happens if — if Justin Rochel marries?'

He paused for so long that she thought he couldn't have heard her and then he said, 'D'you know, I hadn't actually thought of that one. I suppose I see him as a confirmed bachelor!'

'So he doesn't have a — a lady friend?' she asked casually.

'Well now, there is someone — a rather glamorous red-head, but, come to think of it, I only saw her a couple of times — three at the most. Surely if marriage was on the agenda, he'd have said so but, of course, I suppose it wouldn't actually make much difference if he just needed to use Swallowfield as a business base, would it?'

Bethany supposed it was inevitable that a man so very attractive and wealthy as Justin Rochel would have some glamorous female lurking in the background.

'But he might need the money he's going to invest in Swallowfield to buy a house of his own some day,' she persisted.

'We'll cross that bridge when we come to it, shall we? I might need the money to pay to keep me in an old people's home one day, but, in the meantime, our home is secure so let's enjoy it while we may. Anyway, you might be the one to marry . . . '

'That doesn't seem very likely, does it?' she said tartly. 'Wherever would I meet anyone?'

The bookshop was very quiet for the first half hour and so they were able to continue with their conversation.

'I can't quite see how we're going to allocate the rooms, Dad. I know that we don't use all of those upstairs, but we'll still need one for guests.'

'Oh, I'm sure we'll come to some amicable arrangement. Justin is someone who needs his space but the house is big enough to allow him a choice. Actually, I had thought of moving into one of the smaller bedrooms myself — that way, he could have the master bedroom and the adjoining one would make an excellent sitting-room.'

Bethany stared at her father, aghast. 'But you can't — that was Mum's room too. Surely you wouldn't want to move out of it — think of all the memories.'

For an instant his grey eyes — so like her own — were full of pain.

'Sometimes we have to start afresh, Beth,' he said gently. 'Have you ever considered that, perhaps, I would find it easier if I didn't wake up still expecting to find your mother lying beside me?'

Bethany swallowed and reached for his hand. 'Oh, Dad, I'm so sorry. I know how much you miss her . . . I'm being selfish, aren't I?'

'No, of course you're not . . . Now, is there anything else bothering you, darling?'

She sighed. 'It's all so unexpected, that's all. I mean, it's a big step to have a stranger living in the house.'

'Yes, but it's a compromise and, when you get to know him better, I'm sure you'll get on well, Beth. After all, before we knew just how much money we needed to raise, we did

74

discuss taking in a lodger.'

'Yes, but that would have been someone we chose,' she pointed out.

'Well, Justin's chosen us and so I hope we'll make him very welcome.'

She nodded and, realising it was useless to argue any further, fetched him her accounts. He retired to the back room to look over her figures whilst she rearranged a couple of shelves and served an elderly gentleman and a couple of middleaged ladies. Presently, Peter Tyler returned bearing mugs of coffee.

'You've done extremely well. I'm proud of you . . . You know, you're looking tired, Beth, and a bit peaky. How would you feel about having a bit of a holiday when Amber's school term finishes?'

'Where?' As if she didn't know!

'I thought we might all go over to Jersey . . . Obviously, I'd have to return for a short visit before then, but . . . '

Bethany looked at her father in amazement. 'But Dad, you've always said we can't both be away from the shop together. August is one of our busiest periods, remember, and we can't afford to close up then — not even for a week!'

For the next twenty minutes she was kept so busy with a sudden influx of customers that she did not have time to think about this strange proposal. When it had quietened down again Peter Tyler said:

'You see, I've had a lot of time to think recently. I'm not getting any younger and the shop does seem to be pretty tying these days and so I'm considering bowing out — or, at least, only coming in for a few hours a week.'

'Dad, you're not making any sense.' Bethany helped herself to one of Lily's homemade ginger cookies. 'Are you suggesting that I take a holiday in order to fortify me for working here full-time on a permanent basis?'

He laughed. 'No — quite the reverse. I'm thinking of taking on a part-time assistant to help you out. Someone younger than Lily and interested in the trade. It would mean that you and I could go off to auctions together and I could teach you about buying — not that you don't know a fair bit already and . . . '

'Dad, just hold it right there!' She looked at him as if he had gone mad. 'We've barely got enough to pay Lily's wages, let alone anyone else's. You're surely not suggesting we give her the sack, are you? She'd be heartbroken.'

'What? No, of course not — perish the thought. Lily is worth her weight in gold

76

and can stay on here until she no longer wishes to do so.'

'Well that's a relief! So?' she prompted, looking at him expectantly.

'You haven't asked me what I was doing in St. Malo.'

'All right then — so what were you doing in St. Malo?'

He smiled. 'Sophie has some friends living there whom she hadn't seen for a while. They had some visitors staying from America who are interested in purchasing old books and so we were invited over. Sophie had a couple of rather nice volumes of Victor Hugo and well, you know me, I usually manage to have something of interest with me — just in case. I have to say we had a marvellous time . . . '

He paused and Bethany said puzzled, 'Good, but I can't understand where all this is leading.'

'Be patient, darling, I'm coming to that. You see, I think I'm the one who's been rather selfish. Both you girls have made sacrifices recently in order to help out the financial situation. Amber's had to leave her public school — although, I have to say that I think she'll do just as well where she is — and you, my dear Beth, have been working long hours for a pittance, taking no holidays and being what amounts to an unpaid housekeeper into the bargain. Larry Johnson is a wealthy man obsessed by books and so I thought it was about time that I made a sacrifice too.'

Bethany stared at her father, horrified, as she suddenly realised what he must have done. 'Dad, you couldn't have . . . You haven't . . . '

He took her hand. 'Yes, I've promised to sell Larry Johnson most of my collection of first editions. That should ease matters for quite some while.'

Bethany was speechless and, in the end, all she could do was hug her father, knowing that giving up his treasured books was about the hardest thing he could possibly have done — even harder than if he had sold Swallowfield.

4

Bethany put the finishing touches to her flower display and stood back to get the full effect. The theme for the flower festival at St. Cuthbert's that year was 'Caring' and, being one of the last to sign up, she had drawn the short straw and been allocated, 'Friendship' which was quite thought provoking. She had set her spiralling display of delphiniums and yellow roses against a backdrop of bright gold and midnight blue cloth in an attempt to portray sunshine and showers. She had found a beautiful leather bound volume of poetry and opened it at a verse about friends by John Masefield. For her text, she had copied out a verse from Ecclesiasticus Chapter 6:

'A faithful friend is beyond price; his worth is more than money can buy.'

A photograph of herself and friends on graduation day, teardrop earrings and a sepia tint postcard of a picnic completed her display.

'Very effective,' a familiar voice commented

and she spun round to find Justin Rochel watching her from an adjacent pew.

'Mr. Rochel, whenever did you get back? We weren't expecting you until tomorrow.' She felt self conscious, wondering how long he had been there.

'I got through my business in London earlier than I expected and so I decided to come on down. If it's inconvenient I'll stay with the Lomaxes.'

'No — no, not at all.' She tried to remember what Amber had said she was cooking for supper and failed. She just hoped there would be enough. As if reading her thoughts he said:

'I thought if I'd upset the catering we could all go and eat at the local pub.'

She coloured. 'We usually have a well-stocked freezer, Mr. Rochel. Our meals are fairly healthy, but rather simple.'

'Amber was doing something interesting with some tuna when I looked in at Swallowfield.'

'Oh — that's her speciality. Well, if you don't fancy that perhaps you had better eat at the pub . . . Now, if you'll excuse me, I must just tidy up.' She began to pick up the debris. The vicar breezed up to them.

'Charming Bethany. You've done us proud

again, but I don't see any of your lovely paintings.'

'Mags is collecting some of my efforts and setting them up in the village hall . . . You remember Mr. Rochel?'

'Yes, indeed, we met two or three weeks ago, didn't we? Are you staying with Maggie again?'

'No, I shall be putting up at Swallowfield this time.'

Colin Bryce was good at hiding his feelings, but, even so, Bethany thought she detected the slightest flicker of surprise in his kindly blue eyes. 'I see, but of course, didn't young Amber tell me you're a friend of Peter's sister?'

'Yes,' he said briefly and Bethany realised that they would have to tell people their news before long or there would be a lot of unnecessary speculation about what was, she supposed, a rather unusual situation. For the moment, however, she was not in the mood for complicated explanations.

As Justin Rochel drove her the short distance to Swallowfield she said, 'I expect you've come to stake out your claim on the rooms and furniture.'

'Tut, tut, Miss Tyler, what a sharp tongue you have,' he chided, shooting her a look from those Vandyke brown eyes. 'Tell me,

81

has your father mentioned anything about you all visiting Jersey for a holiday?'

'He's mentioned it,' she said dismissively, 'but of course, it's out of the question unless we can get someone to run the bookshop whilst we're away and the only applicants we've had so far have been about eighteen and don't know their Proust from a Mills and Boon.'

He laughed at that. 'I'm sure you'll find someone suitable before long . . . Well, here we are . . . ' He pulled up outside Swallowfield.

Tired after her efforts for the flower festival, she could have done without a house guest as well. Handing Justin Rochel over to her father, she went to see how Amber was progressing with the supper. She fished a fruit pie out of the freezer, opened a can of soup and checked that there were sufficient vegetables to accompany the tuna and pasta bake.

It was strange sitting down to a meal in the dining room instead of eating it round the kitchen table.

'I thought we'd do things properly,' Amber said, 'being it's Justin's first night here.' She saw her sister's disapproving expression. 'You told me to call you, Justin, didn't you?' she appealed to him.

'Certainly I did, on the strength that, although we're not cousins, we might well have been in a different set of circumstances.'

'Don't be ridiculous,' Bethany snapped. 'You know that's just pure fantasy!' She couldn't explain why she felt so angry. It was probably because it seemed as though he was trying to push away the memories of her grandfather and put Cedric Rochel in his place. Amber could be forgiven, for she hadn't known Grandpa Tyler that well, but Bethany had adored the old man and wouldn't allow anyone to say a word against him. So far as she was concerned, any blame for the break up of her grandparents' marriage must rest fairly and squarely with her grandmother.

Peter Tyler gave Bethany a disapproving glance, but Justin wisely chose not to say any more on the subject, recognising that he had better tread carefully if he were to win her over and gain her confidence.

Justin Rochel was very affable, complimenting Amber on the meal and oozing charm from every pore, Bethany thought crossly. She felt she was the only one out of tune with things and resented the way that he had managed to inveigle himself into her family.

A lot had happened during the last three

weeks, but it was going to take quite a bit longer than originally expected before all the legal papers could be drawn up to the satisfaction of all concerned. It was, in fact, a bit of a waiting game.

Justin helped himself to a second portion of pie. 'As we can't do anything for the next few weeks, apart from making a few decisions about the allocation of rooms, alterations etc. why don't you come to Jersey sooner rather than later?'

'The last week of school isn't that important,' Amber said hopefully, passing him the cream.

'Oh, yes it is, young lady. You are not going to miss a single day — so you can completely dismiss that idea,' her father told her firmly.

'I'm sorry to hear you haven't managed to find anyone for the shop yet,' Justin Rochel said.

'Oh, but I have,' Peter Tyler informed them. 'It could work out superbly. An old friend of mine, in the trade, retired recently and I happened to run into him a couple of days back at an auction. He rang me this morning to say that, although he wouldn't want the job on a permanent basis, he'd be more than happy to fill in until we find someone suitable. It would be a much better arrangement to have someone I know managing the shop whilst we're away. Of course, he would want a few less hours, but that's fair enough.'

'So, in theory, there's nothing to prevent you from coming to Jersey just as soon as Amber's term finishes, is there?'

Bethany felt slightly irritated that all the arrangements were being made for her. She suddenly didn't feel in control of the situation any more. After she had helped Amber with the dishes, she took a tray of coffee into the sitting room and found her father and Justin Rochel deep in conversation. He sprang up to take the tray from her.

'I think I'll go down to the village hall for a while to see if Mags needs any help with the exhibition,' she told them.

'Do give her my regards,' Justin said. 'Have you explained to her why I'm staying with you this time?'

'I've just told her you're a friend of Aunt Sophie's and that you're doing some business with my father, and left it at that.'

'Beth doesn't believe in counting her chickens too soon,' Peter Tyler explained and Justin raised his eyebrows.

The village hall was a hive of activity. Besides paintings there were examples of craft work — pottery, needlework, patchwork and tapestry. The following day there would be demonstrations of spinning and lacemaking.

Mags adjusted one of the paintings. 'That's better — I love your poppy picture, Beth.'

Beth was admiring a patchwork cushion cover. 'What? Oh — I only finished that the other day . . . Is this yours, Mags?'

She laughed. 'Yes, my first attempt. I'm so glad I managed to do that course.'

'Is it okay if I come up for an early ride tomorrow, before breakfast?' Bethany asked her friend.

'You know it is . . . It looks like the only chance you'll get this week-end . . . I think the hall is even better than last year, don't you?'

'It's marvellous. Let's hope we get some decent weather to bring out the crowds.'

Mags gathered together her scissors and pens. 'George said he saw Justin Rochel in the village earlier. I thought he wasn't arriving until tomorrow.'

'Oh, he got away a day earlier than expected which is why I'm so late getting down here.'

'He's a bit of a dish, isn't he? I'm surprised he wasn't snapped up long ago.'

'According to my father, he's got a lady friend on Jersey,' Bethany said, in what she hoped was a disinterested tone.

'Really? Oh, what a pity! There's a shortage of eligible single men round here.' Mags darted a mischievous glance at Bethany who was examining some embroidered book covers and did not reply.

The following morning Bethany got up early, dressed in her riding gear and went down to the kitchen to have some tea and a quiet few minutes before anyone else was about. To her annoyance, however, Justin Rochel was already in the kitchen sipping from a mug and looking thoroughly at home.

'Hallo, there's tea in the pot. It's such a beautiful morning, I thought I'd get up early — didn't wake you, did I?'

'Hardly,' she said and poured herself some tea. 'I'm going up to the farm for a ride, so if you want breakfast before I'm back just help yourself. There are plenty of eggs — bacon too if you want it.'

'An early morning ride ... What a wonderful idea! Mind if I join you?'

She was busily spreading honey on a thick slice of bread and butter.

'If you want to, but I can't be long. I've got a busy schedule this morning.' As she sat down she was aware that he was watching her in a way that made her feel disconcerted. 'What's wrong?' she demanded.

'Have I grown two heads in the night or something?'

'I was just thinking how different you look with your hair loose like that.'

She coloured. 'I haven't got round to doing anything with it yet.'

As she made to pass him he caught her arm, and it was as if his very contact set her on fire. 'Come on, Bethany, can't we be friends? What is it that makes you mistrust me so much?'

She shook her arm free, struggling to compose herself.

'My father is a very kind man. He regards everyone as his friend, but he's not always a very good judge of character. Once, a few years ago, he trusted someone who cheated him out of a large sum of money. He was also given some very bad financial advice and, on top of all that, suffered badly in the stockmarket crash of '87, so perhaps you can see why I'm so concerned.'

'Relax, Bethany, I can assure you that I won't let your father down, but if you want to check out my credentials then you're very welcome to do so.'

She shook her head, feeling slightly foolish, and he added gently,

'You're the practical one in the family, aren't you? The one who has to keep her feet on the ground . . . Come on, let's go for that ride.'

It was a beautiful morning and, for a while, as they rode high above the farm, she felt as if she had left all her worries behind her. Justin Rochel seemed so very reassuring. After Toby had left her, she had vowed never to trust any man again, apart from her father. Now, she realised that her memories were not quite so bitter and that the wounds were beginning to heal at last.

As they reached a meadow they set the horses to a canter and, for a moment or two, she forgot that it was her companion who had caused such heartache for her family during the past months. Perhaps she was being unreasonable for, after all, he could hardly be held responsible for the terms of his grandfather's will.

They slowed to a gentle trot as they began the descent down to the village. Below, they could see the church and the postman wending his way along the lane on his bicycle. The air felt fresh and smelt of summer. They passed fields of fast ripening corn strewn with blood-red poppies. Overhead, swallows wheeled. She took a deep breath and began to relax.

'This is the life,' Justin said, but all too soon, they turned into Appleyard Farm and it was time to dismount. Mags appeared, a welcoming smile on her face, as they led the horses back to the field.

'Hallo, Beth, and Mr. Rochel — nice to see you again. It's going to be a glorious day for the flower festival. Are you planning to join us?'

'I might well do this afternoon, but I have to go into Horsham with Peter this morning.' He turned to Bethany and said in an aside, 'He's asked me to go through the accounts for him.'

This was news to Bethany, but then she remembered that Justin Rochel was an accountant, and supposed it made sense that their father would want his ledgers to be accurate, if he were planning to leave the shop in the hands of John Lawrence.

When they arrived back at Swallowfield, Bethany let Justin use the bathroom first as he was the guest and realised what a good idea it would be to have an additional shower room. Her father was already in the study reading his mail.

'Good ride, darling?' he asked looking up with a smile.

She stopped to talk with him for a few minutes and then went upstairs to make the beds wondering what to do about Justin's. His door was open and, peeping in, she saw that he had already made it and that everything was as neat as a new pin.

By the time she had had her shower and come downstairs again she found Justin Rochel cooking bacon and eggs for everyone as naturally as if he had always lived at Swallowfield.

'You should have waited for me,' she said awkwardly.

'Why? I've found everything I wanted. All we need now is your sister.'

Amber appeared a few minutes later looking bleary eyed.

'Goodness — bacon and egg for breakfast! I didn't know you could cook, Justin.'

He placed a laden plate in front of her. 'I can't, apart from breakfasts.'

Amber looked across at Bethany. 'I heard you go out — have you been riding already?'

'Yes, I didn't think you'd want to get up that early. Mr. Rochel and I were out at seven . . . It was wonderful.'

'I'll take your word for it.'

They were clearing the table when the phone rang. Amber came back a few minutes later. 'That was Sarah — she's home for the week-end and she's got Emmy staying with her. She's asked if I can go over and says her father will pick me up from the station at eleven o'clock . . . That's okay, isn't it?'

Her father got to his feet. 'You should have asked first, darling. If you're coming with Justin and me you'd better get a move on. We have to leave in fifteen minutes flat. I've got to see an old lady who wants to part with her entire collection of Beatrix Potter,' and he went out of the room.

'Beth, can't you take me in later?' she appealed.

'No, sorry, I've got to be at the church by eleven for the bellringing demonstration, and then I'm on duty at the vault, after that.'

'The vault?' queried Justin, looking amused.

'Yes — the Carstairs Vault. They used to be the most wealthy landowners around here. Sadly, they've all died out now and the house belongs to a politician who uses it for his country residence. Anyway, the vault still generates a lot of interest on occasions like today.

'Sounds interesting. I must check it out . . . Come on Amber, you won't be that early if you leave now.'

'Okay . . . Well, have fun in your gloomy tomb, Beth,' and she hurried from the kitchen and dashed upstairs to her room.

Bethany said apologetically, 'Amber's had rather a rough time recently. The friends she's meeting are from her public school. She's still missing them and hasn't found it so easy to settle back here.'

Justin looked sympathetic. 'Tough luck — was it the expense?'

'I suppose, in all honesty, it was a combination of factors. My father wasn't too happy about a number of things, but it was certainly the best place for her at the time — with my mother being so ill. The problem is that she's really quite a young fifteen year old and not so worldly as her new classmates.'

'I see . . . So if she's only fifteen then there must be quite a gap between the two of you,' he said curiously.

'She'll be sixteen in August and, if you must know, I'm twenty six. The reason why there's such a big gap is because my brother James died when he was only seven. Had he lived, he would have been twenty-one now.'

There was a pause and then he said, 'I'm sorry, you've obviously had a very distressing time over the years. Don't you have any relations on your mother's side of the family?'

Bethany shook her head. 'No, she was an only child of older parents, both of whom died when I was very small.'

'So why are you so reluctant to accept your Jersey family?'

'I saw my grandmother during her latter

years,' she said defensively, 'but, as for Aunt Sophie — I suppose I find it difficult to understand why she has decided to meet us after all these years, when she's never invited us over before. We've asked her to Swallowfield several times, but she's always made some excuse not to come.'

'Perhaps your aunt feels the same way about the English side of her family as you, apparently, seem to feel about the Jersey side of yours,' he suggested quietly. 'As a matter of fact, it was my suggestion that you all came to Jersey for a holiday but, I can assure you that Sophie was more than happy to go along with it.'

'Of course, it's your house now, isn't it — how could I have forgotten!' she said awkwardly.

He ignored this. 'I feel sure you'll like your Aunt Sophie when you get to know her. Actually, I think you look a bit like her, Bethany. You've both got the same fine bone structure and the same creamy skin . . . I wish you and I could be friends,' he said softly and brushed her cheek gently with his finger, making her want to cry out as a frisson danced down her spine. She told herself that it was because he had caught her unawares that she was reacting in such a strange manner.

'I'm sure you've got plenty of friends back on Jersey,' she said, a trifle unsteadily, the colour staining her cheeks. There was an unfathomable expression in his deep brown eyes.

'That doesn't prevent me from wanting to make new ones, does it?'

She moved away from him, her pulse racing wildly. 'If you'll excuse me — there are one or two things I need to do before going up to the church.'

Whatever was wrong with her? Why didn't she just tell him that she had no intention of going to Jersey? It was as if, in spite of all her misgivings, this man held some kind of attraction for her.

★ ★ ★

The flower festival was going with a swing. There had been over three hundred visitors and it was still only the first day. Bethany was taking yet another party down into the vault when, to her confusion, she realised that Justin Rochel was standing at the back of the group. He seemed to pop up everywhere. She could only pray that she wouldn't lose her concentration.

She began by pointing out the earliest tombs and giving a potted history of the

95

Carstairs family who had arrived in Sussex in the seventeenth century. She kept her eyes averted from Justin, pretending he wasn't there, as she told one or two amusing anecdotes.

A middle-aged man with an untidy beard kept interrupting and asking irrelevant questions, but she managed to keep her cool.

'So how do you know all this?' he asked now, determined to catch her out. She waved a pamphlet at him.

'Oh, I've done my research, believe you me. I've been to the archives, looked up church records and published this little booklet . . . As a matter of fact, the last member of the Carstairs family, who died about a year ago aged ninety, lent me some diaries kept by Isabella Carstairs in the nineteenth century.'

This seemed to shut him up and at the end of her talk he said,

'Ta, very much,' and purchased a copy of her booklet and a couple of postcards of the church. When she finally looked across at Justin Rochel he closed one eye in an almost imperceptible wink, waited until the party was out of earshot and said, 'You were quite magnificent. Tell me, is this really your booklet?'

'Of course . . . It was funded by the local history society and we keep a few copies in the bookshop. I'm planning to do a commentary on Isabella's diaries next and see if I can get those published too.'

'I'm impressed.' He was studying the pamphlet thoughtfully. 'If I told you that I've found some diaries of your grandmother's in the attics of the Jersey house, would you believe me?'

'Why would you make it up?' There was a spark of interest in her grey eyes. She arranged to take a break and he accompanied her to the village hall where teas were being served. He spent quite a while looking at the craft exhibition and, in particular, her paintings.

'You know you've got real talent, Bethany. I'll take any of these that you don't manage to sell back to Jersey with me. I'm convinced there'll be a market for them there.'

When they were seated with cups of tea and a plate of homemade fancies she leant forward, an animated expression on her face.

'So tell me about these diaries belonging to my grandmother.'

'Your aunt and I were going over some things in the attic that had belonged to your grandmother and the diaries were in the bottom of a box, together with some letters Katherine had received from your grandfather. As a matter of fact, we showed them to your father and it was he who suggested you might be interested.'

'Really? It's odd he hasn't mentioned them to me,' she said doubtfully.

'Perhaps he was keeping it as a surprise. He didn't mention your booklet to me either. Bethany, if you came to Jersey you could see the diaries for yourself and there are the most beautiful flowers for you to paint. I'm sure you'd enjoy it, if only you'd come.'

'And what makes you think I won't?' she asked perversely and smiled at him suddenly. 'Justin Rochel, do you really think I want to remain behind when there's still so much I need to know about you and my Aunt Sophie? After all, you have invaded our lives here in Applebourne, so I really don't see why we shouldn't reciprocate and invade yours.'

He laughed at that and put his hand over hers.

'I've never met a girl like you before, Bethany Tyler. You really are quite incorrigible!'

She felt the colour staining her cheeks and said hastily, 'Lily will be pleased. She's got a cousin living on Jersey whom she hasn't heard from recently. I could pay her a visit and find out how she is.'

'Bethany — had you forgotten we're bell-ringing again in five minutes?' a bespectacled young man asked her anxiously.

Bethany, who was miles away, got to her feet, realising how clever Justin Rochel had been, for he had known exactly how to entice her to Jersey.

A few minutes later the bells peeled out mellifluously across the village and Bethany, concentrating hard, had no time to think of the effect the dark-haired visitor from Jersey, sitting listening intently in one of the pews, was having on her emotions.

That night she reflected that it had been a pleasant day and that, perhaps things wouldn't be quite so difficult from now on. After Toby had announced his engagement to Dianne, Bethany had been determined not to get involved with any man ever again, but when Justin Rochel had walked into her life, unannounced, a few weeks ago, he had managed to awaken her to the realisation that she was leading a dull and uneventful existence. The prospect of a couple of weeks in Jersey filled her with sudden hope. Perhaps she could begin to enjoy life again. Suddenly, she knew that she wanted to meet Aunt Sophie and to see Justin Rochel in his home environment.

Justin met them at Jersey airport and whisked them off to his waiting Rolls which was sleek, silver and gleaming. Peter Tyler had told them very little about the house where Aunt Sophie and Justin lived, probably because he just accepted his surroundings, being equally at home in a mansion or a shack. He was so vague about things, at times, that he could be rather exasperating, but it was one of his few failings and rather endearing.

'I don't know whether your father has told you, but Lilyville is actually in the parish of St. Peter, although we're nearly into St. Ouen.'

'Oh, Daddy never remembers to tell us anything like that,' Amber informed him. 'Anyway, we ought to remember with him being called Peter.'

Peter Tyler laughed. 'D'you know, I've never thought of that . . . How's Sophie, Justin?'

'Oh, her usual self — pleased that you're returning so soon.'

Bethany looked out of the window with quiet pleasure as they were driven along leafy lanes, past fields where tan-coloured Jersey cows grazed. Nothing, however, could have prepared her for Lilyville, for the elegant white house was more like a mansion. Swallowfield, which had always seemed spacious to her, would have fitted into it several times over.

Justin parked precisely and they got out. Amber and Bethany stood gazing about them in sheer delight at the beautifully tended gardens and complete tranquillity of the place.

'Come on in,' he said. 'Sophie will have heard the car and be wondering what's keeping us.'

Amber and Bethany scarcely had time to take in their surroundings — merely receiving an impression of spaciousness and luxury — before they were ushered into a sitting-room which was all pale green and white with antique furniture and deep carpets.

Sophie Le Claire stood waiting to greet them — a tall rather plump figure with brown hair streaked with silver who did look, Bethany had to concede, a little like an older edition of herself. She was dressed in a silky pink dress that no doubt bore a designer label.

'I've waited a long time for this,' she said huskily. 'You can't know how pleased I am to have my family around me at last . . . Justin has told me so much about you. Peter, thank you for coming back and bringing your daughters with you.' She greeted Amber with a kiss and than turning to Bethany said, 'They tell me, Bethany, that you look like me, but you will need to put a little more flesh on those bones — still I daresay some of our Jersey cream will do the trick . . . Welcome to Lilyville, my dears.'

Bethany was wearing a new dress that Mags had helped her to choose — a pale green print that suited her colouring well, her fine brown hair was neatly confined in a french pleat and she had on the lightest of make-up. She had the feeling that Aunt Sophie had taken in every detail of her appearance and hoped that she met with her approval.

Amber was looking out of the window. 'How far is the sea?' she wanted to know.

'Oh, not too far, but if you're thinking of swimming then we've got our own pool. The sea isn't the best for swimming in. It can be rather rough, but the beaches are quite something.'

Amber started at Justin. 'How fabulous to have your own pool! When can I use it?'

'Hold on,' her father said. 'You've got plenty of time. We've only just arrived.'

After tea they went upstairs to unpack. The bedrooms were tastefully decorated and had everything they could possibly wish for including ensuite bathrooms. As she hung up her dresses, Bethany couldn't help feeling rather like the poor relation and then realised that they had had to sell off half of Swallowfield in order to finance Aunt Sophie in this lifestyle. As for Justin, he must be exceptionlly wealthy to afford the upkeep of such a large house as Lilyville.

Presently, she decided to go in search of Amber, but voices drifting up from the garden told her that that young lady was already making herself at home and was obviously getting Justin to show her round.

Making her way downstairs, Bethany found her father having a well deserved nap in a lounger on the terrace and, unsure what to do, went back into the house again.

'Hallo my dear.' She started for Aunt Sophie had been so quiet that she had not noticed her standing there in the hall.

'Won't you come into the sitting-room and talk to me for a while? I'd like to get to know you. We usually dine at seven, but tonight I've arranged for us to eat at six thirty.'

They sat together on the pale green sofa and Sophie said, 'Well this is nice. Justin thought you might not agree to come, but he always was persuasive and here you are. I hope you'll have a happy stay. This is such a beautiful island . . . Justin tells me you've had quite a rough time of it recently.'

'All families have their problem patches, Aunt Sophie. We'll get through it, no doubt.'

'Yes, it can't have been easy for you, but, at least, now that Justin has put up the money for half of Swallowfield, that should solve one problem.'

Aunt Sophie made it sound as if Justin were doing them a favour and it had nothing to do with her, Bethany thought. But if she hadn't been so desperately in need of her share of the capital, then the situation wouldn't have arisen in the first place.

'I just hope Mr. Rochel is happy with the arrangement,' Bethany said carefully. 'After all, sharing a house with comparative strangers is not the easiest thing in the world to do.'

'Quite.' Sophie gave a little smile and Bethany realised that that, of course, was exactly what her Aunt and Justin would be doing for the next fortnight.

'It really was most kind of you to invite us,' she said hastily.

'Nonsense — I wanted to meet you all. It seemed so silly to have relations in England and never to have seen them. Now that we have rectified the situation, well I can't imagine why it didn't happen years back. Of course, Justin, dear boy, has been such a tower of strength since Cedric died. All I can hope for is that we can all get on well together, and that will make me a very happy woman . . . I know that Justin was very impressed with Swallowfield.'

'You would be more than welcome to visit us there,' Bethany told her.

'No — no, my dear. I'm quite happy here in my own little world with just the occasional trip to the other islands or St. Malo, but I'm glad Justin has taken to Swallowfield. He tells me he likes what he's seen of Applebourne and, once he's got things as he wants them in the house, then he's planning to spend quite a bit of time there.'

'How do you mean — 'got things as he wants them' ? ' Bethany queried frowningly.

Her aunt smoothed her dress. 'Well, he'll naturally want to make one or two alterations in order to have his own self-contained apartment. He tells me you've only got one bathroom at present.'

'And a downstairs cloakroom,' Bethany said defensively.

'But now that there's going to be four of you that situation must be remedied — and the kitchen facilities need updating, I gather. Justin is used to modern appliances — a microwave, dishwasher — that sort of thing.'

A growing resentment against Justin Rochel burnt inside her. He had obviously not wasted any time in discussing the shortcomings of Swallowfield with Sophie.

'He knew what he was taking on,' she pointed out, 'and he seemed fairly satisfied with everything at the time. If he doesn't like it then he's still got time to pull out — the legal documents haven't been finalised yet.'

'Oh, but they have,' her aunt told her quietly. 'The letter arrived in today's post. Justin has contacts and knows how to put pressure on our solicitors. Now it's completely official. Justin owns a half share in Swallowfield!'

5

For the first few moments after waking, Bethany could not remember where she was. The sun streamed goldenly through the curtains and she realised that she had slept longer than she had intended. After a quick shower, she dressed in a turquoise cotton skirt and sleeveless white top and went down to breakfast.

Amber was tucking into a bowl of cereal. 'Isn't this a brilliant place! Justin and I have been for a swim already . . . It's not like you to sleep in, Beth. Are you okay?'

Bethany assured her that she was and helped herself to a glass of orange juice. A moment or two later Justin and her father appeared followed by a rather stout, middle-aged lady in a floral pinafore who introduced herself as 'Mrs. Vibert,' and asked if they would all like a cooked breakfast. It seemed that Sophie always took breakfast in her room.

'Your father and aunt are off to St. Helier this morning,' Justin told Bethany presently, 'and I've arranged to take Amber over to St. Ouen if you'd care to join us. Some mutual friends of Sophie and myself have got their grandchildren staying. They're about Amber's age and I thought it would be company for her.'

Bethany quite expected Amber to protest, remembering similar attempts they had made to find friends for her in the past. She had made it plain that she preferred to find her own, thank you very much. To Bethany's surprise, however, Amber seemed perfectly happy with the arrangement which she and Justin had obviously discussed earlier.

'It sounds fine to me,' Bethany said and looked across at her father. She hadn't had an opportunity to speak with him alone, since the conversation she had had with Sophie the previous evening. She had the oddest feeling that he was avoiding her. There was the tiniest niggle of doubt, at the back of her mind, that things were not quite so straightforward as she would have liked regarding the transaction with Swallowfield.

'Is that okay with you, Beth?' Peter Tyler asked. 'Your aunt and I have a couple of matters to attend to in St. Helier and then we're visiting some friends of hers in St. Aubin . . . Of course, you'd be more than welcome to come with us . . . '

'No, no, I'll go with Amber and Mr. Rochel — you enjoy your morning.' She turned to

108

Justin. 'It's kind of you to entertain us, but don't you have to go to work?'

'No, not today . . . I'm pretty much self-employed these days and often work from home, but I've decided to have a few days holiday in honour of your company . . . Come on, I'll show you my office.' He led them upstairs and flung open a door at the end of a corridor. The room was equipped with everything he could possibly want from a fax machine and computer to book-lined shelves and filing cabinet.

'Whow,' said Amber, taking a closer look at the computer. 'I expect you'll need a room like this at Swallowfield for when you have business to do there?' She had asked the very question that Bethany had been burning to ask.

'Well, not quite so well equipped as this perhaps, but, yes, I'll need something similar . . . Anyway, we can discuss that later.'

'That means you'll be wanting one of the ground floor rooms, I suppose?' Bethany enquired.

He switched on his answer-phone. 'All in good time. So far we've only talked about two of the bedrooms being converted for my use, if you remember . . . By the way, has your father told you that my side of things is settled now? Aren't you going to welcome me

109

as a member of your household at last?'

For answer Amber hugged him. 'It'll be like having a very nice cousin to stay,' she told him and planted a kiss on his cheek. For a moment he looked startled and then he chuckled.

'Well, thanks . . . and you, Bethany, aren't you at least going to shake my hand?'

Bethany was saved from replying by Aunt Sophie's voice calling Justin imperiously from somewhere along the corridor. He excused himself and disappeared for a few moments leaving Amber to say:

'Isn't this room fab? Justin says we can go riding some time — and wasn't it brilliant of him to arrange for me to meet up with his friends' grandchildren this morning?'

'Yes, very nice,' Bethany said absently. It seemed as though they were all fixed up except for her. Her father had already joined Sophie's social set and Amber was obviously going to be doing the same. Oh well, Bethany supposed she could always go off and explore on her own, providing, of course, that Lilyville was on a bus route.

Justin came from Sophie's room looking a little disconcerted. He didn't say anything, however, until they were climbing the second flight of stairs to their own rooms.

'I had hoped we could have this week to

ourselves before Sophie started entertaining, but she's anxious to show you off and so she's decided to throw one of her dinner parties on Saturday. Apparently, she's already invited most of the guests before thinking to mention it to me.'

'Am I invited?' Amber asked anxiously. 'Whatever shall I wear?'

He ruffled her hair. 'Oh, don't worry about that. We can always get you something in St. Helier if you haven't anything suitable . . . They do tend to be a bit formal.'

'You should have warned us,' Bethany protested indignantly. As it happened, she had packed a couple of formal dresses, just in case, but she hadn't reckoned on anything too grand and Amber would definitely need something new. This holiday was going to prove more expensive than she had bargained for. They parted at Amber's door.

'Bring your sketch book,' Justin told Bethany. 'We might find some wild flowers for you to draw.'

When she had collected her cardigan and flung a few things into her tapestry shoulder bag, Bethany went in search of her father. She found him reading a newspaper on the terrace.

'Dad, did you know that Justin Rochel is aiming to turn one of our downstairs rooms

111

into an office and make countless alterations to the house so that he can have a self-contained apartment? And as he's already having two of the upstairs rooms, wherever would we sleep visitors?'

Peter Tyler put down his newspaper. 'Bethany, my dear, you do seem to be forseeing problems that don't exist. If you remember, we've already talked about updating the kitchen and putting in a shower room and, I thought, you seemed quite happy about it then . . . If we have visitors when Justin isn't at Swallowfield then, he has told me, we can use his bedroom and, if he is there and it's a friend of Amber's then I'm sure she'll share.'

'And, what if it's a friend of mine or yours?'

He sighed. 'When your grandfather was alive, I can remember Christmasses before the attics were converted, when we put camp beds all over the place . . . It's a big enough house and we can always get a bed settee so do stop troubling yourself. I thought you would have been pleased that the paperwork has been completed more quickly than we anticipated.'

He made to pick up his newspaper, but Bethany firmly removed it.

'And, another thing — did you know

that your sister is giving a dinner party on Saturday? I don't expect you've brought your dinner jacket with you, have you?'

'I'll hire one in St. Helier and you girls can go shopping if you need new frocks . . . Now just go off and enjoy yourself, darling. We'll get by, you'll see.'

And Bethany, realising that it would be useless to pursue the conversation any longer, went into the hall to wait for Justin and Amber.

The Vautiers turned out to be a delightful family. Within minutes of meeting up, the grandchildren, Charlotte and James, had carted Amber off to the beach cafe for cokes whilst the older members of the party enjoyed coffee on the terrace of a nearby hotel. It evolved that Rupert and Olivia Vautier owned a yacht and Bethany realised that the promise of a trip along the coast had obviously been the attraction so far as Amber was concerned.

'We'll see you later,' Justin said after about half an hour.

'You'd be more than welcome to join us,' Olivia Vautier offered, but Justin declined the invitation politely, and Bethany, following him down the steps and out into the sunshine wondered what was on the agenda now.

'We're going off for a coastal ride,' he

informed her and, although part of her wanted to tell him that she would have appreciated being consulted first, her heart missed a beat at the thought of being alone with him. He had obviously engineered this trip and she was beginning to recognise that he was a man who liked to be in control and make decisions.

'We'll take a look at Grosnez Point, first of all,' he said. 'You'll get a spectacular view from there.'

And he was right. Grosnez Point was at the north-west corner of the island. She stood on the heather and gorse clad granite cliffs tasting the salt spray. He took her arm as if it were the most natural thing in the world to do.

'Look, you can see right across to Guernsey and Sark from here and over there are the remains of a castle said to be fourteenth century, that's been the subject for several paintings . . . There are masses of wild flowers along this coastline — Sea Stock, Samphire and the Yellow Horned Poppy to name but a few . . . Did you bring your sketch book?'

She shook her head. 'Not today, but I will another time.'

Next they went to Plemont Bay where she delighted in the silver sand and the caves cut deeply from the steep cliffs. Again there were clear views across to the other islands. Justin pointed out the well-known Needle Rock.

'There's so much I want to show you,' he said, 'but I think perhaps one more stop and then lunch.'

She wasn't clear how it happened, but suddenly he had slipped a casual arm about her waist and they were laughing and talking together as easily as if they had been lovers. He seemed so different here in Jersey that she almost forgot her reasons for mistrusting him.

Parking the car at St. Mary, they stopped to look at the church and then decided that, as neither of them were hungry, they would continue to Grève de Lecq. It was an enchanting walk through a leafy wooded valley and when they eventually ended up at Grève de Lecq, he was rewarded by her intake of breath. It was a delightful cove. Here the cliffs were grassy and the sand a deeper, richer colour. For a time they sat in silence watching the sunlight on the sea and the expanse of blue sky beyond.

'I could stay here all day,' she told him, closing her eyes, and for answer he leant across and kissed her gently on the mouth. The kiss was as light as thistledown so that, for a moment, she wondered if she could

115

have dreamt it, but when she opened her eyes, the expression in his own dark brown ones told her that it had been real enough and her heart sang.

Presently they went to have a cold drink at a nearby café before slowly retracing their steps through the valley.

'I shall be in trouble from Sophie for wearing you out,' he said as they had a late lunch in one of the local pubs.

She smiled at him. 'But I've loved every minute of it.'

He returned her smile. 'Then I'll make no apology for kissing you.'

Her heart felt lighter than it had for months and, suddenly, she was aware of emotions that had long been buried.

As they sat drinking coffee and chatting about everything in general, she felt a strange contentment wash over her. How could she have doubted this kind, gentle man? She was sure that they were on the brink of a new relationship — one that could only get better. Suddenly, however, he glanced at his watch and got to his feet.

'I'm afraid we'll have to be going. I hadn't realised it was quite so late and I've a dinner engagement this evening.'

She was irrationally disappointed, for she had wanted the day to go on forever. He

116

was silent most of the way home and she contented herself by watching the tranquil scenery and reliving the time they had spent together. Once or twice she stole a look at him. She had been told that Jersey men were not particularly handsome, but she found him extremely attractive with his near-black hair and tanned skin and those wonderful deep brown eyes. She knew he had some Irish blood in him on his mother's side. She wondered why she had been so suspicious of him at first and supposed it was because, after her experience with Toby, she had found it difficult to trust any man. She wondered who he was dining with that night and suddenly remembered the red-headed woman friend that her father had mentioned and felt an odd pang of jealousy, alien to her nature.

When they arrived back at Lilyville, Justin thanked her rather politely for her company and disappeared in the direction of his office. Staring after him, she felt that there had been a dream-like quality about the day.

Sophie came from the kitchen looking surprised to see her.

'Hallo, I thought I heard voices. Did you have a good time, my dear? You're back rather early. I quite thought you'd gone sailing with the Vautiers.'

'No, Justin took me sight-seeing, but he's had to get back because he's going out to dinner. The Vautiers are bringing Amber back later.'

Sophie's face was expressionless, but there was something about her eyes that told Bethany that for some reason she had not expected this answer.

'I see — Justin is so popular that it's a wonder he's free on Saturday. I've invited twelve for dinner, by the way . . . I'm concerned for your young sister. I think she might be bored.'

'On the contrary, I'm sure she'll feel very grown up,' Bethany assured her aunt.

'Well, let's hope so — there seems so much to think about.'

'Perhaps I can help in some way.' Bethany felt uncomfortably aware that her aunt was putting herself out on her family's account.

'Oh, no, my dear,' Sophie sounded quite shocked. 'You're a guest — I simply wouldn't hear of it. Anyway, I've got a couple of local women coming in to help Mrs. Vibert and Nicki. I always make the sauces and desserts myself and supervise generally. Fortunately, I enjoy cooking.'

In the event, the problem concerning Amber resolved itself for that young lady had had a marvellous time with the Vautiers and wanted to know if she could go to James' sixteenth birthday party on board the yacht that Saturday.

Aunt Sophie said, 'Of course you may. It'll be far more fun for you, I'm sure. Just so long as you promise to be back in time to meet my guests before they leave.'

The following morning, the Vautiers called by to see if Amber wanted to spend the day with them again. An ecstatic Amber rushed off to collect her things with Charlotte and James in tow. Sophie, always the social hostess, organised coffee and soft drinks on the terrace which Bethany had a feeling they could have done without. She was, however, pleased to see Amber looking so happy.

Having waved them goodbye, Sophie announced that she was expecting guests for lunch and, refusing Bethany's offer of help, went into the kitchen to see Mrs. Vibert.

'If you're at a loose end, Bethany, why don't you come with me' Justin suggested. 'Sophie's asked me to pick up some table wine. We could turn it into an excursion and I'll take you to La Mare Vineyard.'

'I did promise Lily I'd go to see her cousin and deliver the sweater she's knitted for her, but I don't suppose there'd be time before lunch?'

Justin consulted his watch. 'Not really,

as we would need to be back around one o'clock. I tell you what, I could always run you over there this afternoon . . . Come on, let's beat a hasty retreat before anyone else shows up.'

Bethany was captivated by La Mare Vineyards which were set in the heart of the tranquil Jersey countryside in St. Mary, surrounding a charming old farmhouse with peaceful orchards and gardens.

'This was Jersey's first winery,' Justin informed her, and casually taking her arm, led her into the vineyard where she stood entranced. There was something about the place that had a romantic quality.

'We haven't got time for the full tour this morning, but we can always come back here. I just wanted you to see what there was on offer. They produce cider here too. They've got a wonderful press which they use each autumn. There's actually been a local cider-making industry on Jersey since the 1760s and, at one time, half the land on the island was used for growing the apples. Of course, in those days, they used a horse to pull the wheel operating the cider press . . . So what do you think then?'

'It's beautiful, Justin,' she enthused and was rewarded by his smile which made him seem rather boyish and, as they were completely alone, apart from the birds, he bent and kissed her lightly on the mouth.

'Did anyone tell you, you have the most irresistible mouth, Bethany Tyler!'

She felt herself trembling at his closeness and wanted him to kiss her properly. Instead he said, 'Come on, let's go and sample the wine.'

Presently they sat enjoying glasses of the delicious fruity Clos de la Mare white wine, of which he had purchased several bottles.

'This is bliss,' she told him, sipping her drink appreciatively, and he chuckled.

'Ah, now you are beginning to unwind. Next time you can try the Clos de Seyval which is slightly sweet . . . Now, much as I'd enjoy staying here for the rest of the day, we'll have to make tracks soon or Sophie will be champing at the bit.'

'You're very good to her, Justin.'

He shrugged. 'That's because she's been very good to me. She looked after me when I was at my most vulnerable and now the opportunity has come for me to repay some of her kindness. It's a role reversal, if you like.'

'You know, you're very different from how I thought you were when we first met.'

He laughed. 'I seem to remember you viewed me with the utmost suspicion then — was that really less than a couple of months ago?'

'If you had told me then that I'd be sitting with you here today, I wouldn't have believed you.'

He reached across and touched her hand and she set down her glass before she spilt the contents. There was a chemistry between them and she was powerless to do anything about it. For a few moments they sat in companionable silence and then he got to his feet.

'Regretfully we have to be making a move . . . If we can get away from the luncheon party we can still go to see Lily's cousin this afternoon. I wouldn't be surprised if Sophie's friends leave around three thirty. They're great golfing enthusiasts.'

'Sophie seems to have a great many friends,' she commented.

He nodded. 'Yes, she's a very popular person — kind, generous to a fault — mind you, she does rather like her own way, but remember, she's been used to ruling the roost. Cedric adored her and treated her as if she were his own daughter.'

'Could that be why her marriage didn't work — because she wasn't prepared to allow for give and take?'

She saw the slight frown furrowing his brow and thought she had better not pursue the subject, not wanting to spoil what had been a beautiful morning.

'Sophie's husband was no good to her — a ne'er do well, to coin an old fashioned expression. They were hopelessly in love for the first few years, but then his attention wandered. He went abroad on business and met someone else. Sophie took it very badly — for her, marriage is for life. She had already suffered as a child, when she believed that her own father had rejected her, and so her experience of men has not been good.'

'Thank you for explaining that, Justin. It's helped me to understand things a lot better.' If only he had said all this to her before. She wondered how much of Sophie's suffering her father was aware of. 'Anyway I'm sure you and Cedric have made up for all her previous unhappiness.'

'We've tried and now your father and you and Amber are here making her feel that she's got a family of her own once again. I know that Cedric hoped that she would find some nice man with whom she could spend the rest of her days, but it wasn't to be.'

Aunt Sophie had that in common with herself, thought Bethany rather bitterly, for they had both been thwarted in love.

As Justin had predicted, Sophie's friends departed around three thirty and she announced that she was feeling rather tired and was going for a lie down.

Peter Tyler settled himself comfortably on the terrace with an impressive book on Jersey. Bethany had the distinct feeling that he might be deliberately throwing Justin and herself into each other's company, as normally he would have opted to come with them to visit Lily's cousin, Marjorie Touzel.

Justin suggested that Bethany might care to take some flowers from the garden for the old lady, and she decided that this just indicated what a thoughtful person he was.

'We do seem to be seeing rather a lot of St. Mary,' he said presently, as he parked the car outside a row of typical granite houses.

At first there was no reply to his knock, but eventually a sharp-faced woman in an expensive looking linen suit appeared.

'Yes?' she enquired.

Without preamble, Justin explained who they were and why they were there. It appeared that the woman was Lily's cousin's daughter-in-law. She seemed reluctant to let them see her mother-in-law at first but then, that lady, hearing their voices, called out:

'Who is it, Rita?' The woman hesitated and then said ungraciously:

'I suppose you'd better come in for a few minutes,' and led the way into a comfortable, but rather old-fashioned sitting-room.

After introductions had been made, Marjorie Touzel's face creased in smiles. 'Of course, I remember you now, Miss Tyler. We met last time I stayed in Applebourne, didn't we?' She turned to Justin.

'And you, Mr. Rochel — I knew your grandfather well . . . So what do you think of Jersey then, Miss Tyler?'

'I only arrived a few days ago but, from what I've seen of it so far, it's very beautiful.'

Bethany was aware that Rita Touzel seemed reluctant to leave the room, although judging from her impatient manner she obviously had other things to do. Perhaps she was just curious or was she afraid that her mother-in-law might say something out of turn?

'How's Lily?' Marjorie Touzel asked, sniffing the flowers Bethany had given her, appreciatively.

'Oh, she's fine, but she's been rather worried because she hasn't heard from you for such a long time.'

'My mother-in-law has been very busy lately,' Rita Touzel snapped, 'and she's got arthritis which makes writing difficult.'

'Only sometimes when it's playing up. We have been busy though since my son and daughter-in-law moved in with me. I'm sorry

Lily's been worried. Perhaps you can tell her there's no need and that I'll be in touch soon . . . It's so kind of you to take the trouble to call.'

'Lily's made you a jumper,' Bethany said, producing the parcel. 'She knows you like this pattern because it's similar to the one she made for herself which you admired. She hopes you like the colour.'

'I used to do lots of knitting before my hands got bad, but I was never so good as Lily.' The old lady undid the parcel eagerly. 'Oh look, Rita, isn't that lovely!'

'Very nice, I'm sure, although you've got plenty of woollies,' said Rita Touzel. She looked rather pointedly at the clock and it was obvious she was not going to offer them any tea.

They spent a few more minutes chatting and then Justin said, 'Well we'd best be getting back. It's been delightful talking with you.'

Marjorie Touzel looked disappointed but her daughter-in-law was already heading for the door. Justin followed her out into the hall, but Bethany lingered, and taking the old lady's hand said quietly:

'We'll call again if that's all right?'

'Please do,' she said and then lowering her voice added, 'Come on a Tuesday or Friday morning. Rita goes shopping then and we can have a bit of a chat.'

Bethany nodded conspiratorially. Justin was waiting for her outside in the sunshine. 'So what did you make of all that?'

'There's something not quite right about the situation.' She told him what Marjorie Touzel had said to her as she was leaving.

'Hmn — she obviously wants the opportunity to speak with you alone. Personally, I can't say I cared overmuch for the daughter-in-law's attitude.'

'No, it was as if she couldn't wait to get rid of us, but, perhaps, we just called at the wrong time. For Lily's sake I must make sure that her cousin really is all right. There was something I couldn't quite put my finger on . . .'

He nodded. 'I'm inclined to agree with you. However, we can't do anything more for the moment . . . Now, I don't know about you, but I could definitely do with a cup of tea!'

They found a small teashop a short drive away. It was almost closing time and so they had the place practically to themselves. The proprietor served them with a welcome pot of tea and a plate of homemade scones with cream and jam.

Over tea, they discussed Marjorie Touzel's

situation more fully. By now, Bethany was convinced that all was not well in that household.

'Don't worry, if there is a problem then I'm sure we'll find out before long,' Justin assured her. 'Is it true what you told Marjorie Touzel about your first impressions of Jersey? Do you really think it's a beautiful island?'

'Yes, I do,' she said sincerely, 'and it's making such a change for me, being here. You see, I think I've been content to be in Applebourne for so long that I was beginning to forget there's a big wide world out there just waiting to be explored.'

He smiled and caught her hand in his. 'And I'm going to take great pleasure in exploring this little island with you and showing you all my favourite haunts.'

And she felt a surge of happiness at the prospect of spending even more time with him. He smiled as if he could see into her heart.

'I've got a special treat lined up for you tomorrow afternoon for a start.'

'What is it?' she demanded.

Justin laughed at her childlike enthusiasm. 'You'll just have to be patient and wait and see, won't you? Now are you going to eat that last scone or shall I?'

6

The gardens at Lilyville were beautiful, full of bright, fragrant blooms, tropical plants and palms. Bethany had discovered a small pagoda-shaped summer house and, early the next morning, she settled to her painting. She felt relaxed and full of inspiration. Amber, returning from a swim, stopped to speak with her.

'Honestly Beth, fancy shutting yourself away in here when you could be enjoying yourself in the pool. You can paint at home!'

'Not blooms like these, you can't.' She indicated the lilies on the bench beside her. 'It's all right, I haven't picked them — just filched them from a vase in the hall . . . For your information, little sister, I have been swimming. I went the other afternoon when you were out with the Vautiers. Anyway, you're obviously enjoying yourself.'

Amber shook herself and droplets of water fell off like raindrops.

'It's brill and, later on, Justin's driving me to St. Brelade to meet up with James and Charlotte. We're going wind-surfing.'

Bethany set down her brushes. 'But you can't wind-surf.'

'I'm having lessons,' Amber informed her triumphantly.

'It's the first I've heard of it. Amber, lessons are expensive and you know we're on rather a tight budget at the moment.'

Amber rubbed her hair with a corner of the towel.

'It's okay — Justin's paying.'

Bethany, taken aback, stared at her. 'For goodness sake, Amber, we can't go taking money from Justin. I'll have to speak to him.'

Amber looked petulant. 'He said it was a present, because he wants to think of us as his family — don't go spoiling everything! Why do you always have to, Bethany Tyler!' And she raced off across the lawn nearly colliding with Justin who was coming from the terrace. A few moments later he entered the summer house.

'I thought I'd find you in here. So what's wrong with young Amber? Have you two had words?'

'You know perfectly well what's wrong if you've just asked her!' she replied testily. 'I am fully aware of the cost of wind-surfing lessons and we can't allow you to pay . . . We're not a charity, you know!'

'Far from it. You know you are such a proud person, Bethany. If it had been Sophie or your grandmother instead of yourself they wouldn't have thought twice about accepting my gift, but . . . '

'My father and I prefer to pay our own way, and if we can't then we go without,' she said tartly.

'All right then — look at it from my angle. I suddenly find myself with a ready made family and so, is it any wonder that I want to give them presents to compensate for all the Christmasses and birthdays I've missed over the years?'

Bethany said furiously, 'Let's get one or two things straight. We are not and never have been your family, because my grandmother never divorced my grandfather. They died man and wife, in spite of what you may have wished.'

He spread his hands. 'True, but Katherine called herself 'Rochel' and she requested that she wanted to be buried here — not in Applebourne with your grandfather . . . '

'Did you have to remind me of that?' Bethany practically yelled at him.

'And now, Cedric has been buried beside her in what many would consider to be his rightful place,' he added, ignoring her.

Bethany picked up her paintbrush and

added a few details to the lily, trying to compose herself. He knew her Achilles heel all right.

'Anyway, if you had really wanted to help us then why couldn't you have simply advanced the money to Aunt Sophie from your capital, as a sort of trust fund, instead of turning both Swallowfield and our lives upside down?'

She saw the look of incredulity on his face and immediately wished she could retract the remark, aware that she was being unreasonable.

'I thought you were happy with the arrangement, but it would seem that I just can't win.'

She shook her head as if to clear her mind. 'Justin — I'm sorry. It's just that . . . '

His brown eyes flashed. 'That you can't bear the thought of me living under the same roof as you, is that it?'

'No!' she said desperately, feeling confused by her emotions. 'I just don't understand that's all.'

He sighed. 'Then we'll run through it all again, shall we? Sophie isn't good with money as I've told you before. I don't wish to sound disloyal but the plain fact is that she's never had to be. For years there's always been someone to pick up the bills. She probably won't be able to resist spending some of the capital I've invested for her anyway, but at least I've made it more difficult for her to get at and I've still got a half share in Swallowfield as collateral — if we like to think of it in that way — so there will always be something left at the end of the day!'

Bethany tried to understand his reasoning, recognising that it would be difficult for Aunt Sophie to learn to economise at this stage of her life, but finding it hard to believe that she was really so extravagant as Justin made out.

'I can quite see why Aunt Sophie would want to sell her share in Swallowfield,' she said at last. 'I know she's got to look to the future and realise she needs capital of her own in order to remain independent.'

He nodded. 'And I promised my grandfather I'd look after Sophie.'

'But what about her husband? Surely he's got some financial responsibility towards her?'

Justin shrugged. 'Oh, he's living on the other side of the Atlantic, I believe, and so it's no good relying on him to support her . . . Anyway, they are divorced now, but don't ever mention it to Sophie because she finds it much too upsetting. You're like her in so many ways, Bethany — sensitive, perceptive.'

She managed a little smile. 'But not extravagant.'

He grinned wrily. 'No, and if I've offended you by paying for Amber's lessons then I'm sorry. Of course, we could always reach a compromise.'

'How?' He reached into his pocket and bringing out a leather wallet removed some Jersey notes which he put on the seat beside her.

'I've been waiting for the right moment to talk to you about this. You remember I took a few of your pictures back with me?'

'Yes,' she said puzzled. 'The ones that didn't sell at the flower festival.'

'A friend of mine put them in his shop and they sold within a week so that money's yours, Bethany. There are lots of tourists on this island — many of them wealthy and looking for original works to impress their friends and relatives. Paul's taken a 5% commission on this occasion and the cost of the frames, so I hope that's satisfactory.'

'Wow!' Bethany exclaimed, elated. 'That's a pleasant surprise.'

He stood behind her, his hands casually resting on her shoulders as he studied her painting. 'That's beautiful. I was going to suggest that you tried something with a Jersey flavour, but you've already done so, and, when you get tired of painting lilies, then there are all the wild flowers on the island . . . So, you see if you really want to pay something towards Amber's lessons, now you have the means of doing it.'

His hands on her shoulders felt as if they were scorching her skin and a tiny frisson danced down her spine at his closeness.

'I don't know what to say — everything's happening so fast.'

Catching her hands he pulled her to her feet and, before she realised his intention, he said, 'And what about this — is this too fast for you too?' And his lips came down on hers, taking her breath away.

It was a long lingering kiss that sent her senses reeling. She could feel the warmth of his muscular body against her and wanted to cry out. Reaching up she entwined her fingers in his thick, dark hair. She was not to know that at that precise moment Sophie, who was about early that morning and looking for Justin, stopped by the entrance to the summer house and glanced in. Bethany would have found the disapproving look on her aunt's face disconcerting, but immersed in an enchanted, faraway world where everything was beautiful, she was blissfully unaware of it.

Bethany completed her lily painting that morning. Sophie was a little cool in her manner towards her at lunch, but Bethany thought perhaps her aunt had something on her mind and didn't associate it with anything she might have done to upset her.

'Your father and I are going to St. Brelade this afternoon, would you like to come with us?' Sophie asked her niece presently.

'I would have enjoyed that, but Justin's arranged for us to go riding.'

Sophie looked put out. 'He didn't mention it to me. I quite thought he was tied up for the rest of the day. Oh well, never mind. There's always another time, I suppose.'

Bethany caught the disappointment in her aunt's voice and for some reason felt guilty. She resolved to spend more time with her during the rest of her stay.

'I wanted to show you some more of our beautiful countryside,' Justin told Bethany as he drove them to Trinity later that afternoon. 'We usually have to stay in an escorted ride, so I hope you won't find it too restricting.'

The memory of his kisses were still fresh in her memory and she wanted to tell him that so long as she was with him it wouldn't matter.

It was good to be in the saddle again and it was a wonderful ride along quiet leafy country lanes.

'One morning we'll book in an early ride on the beach. Have you ever ridden on sand?'

She shook her head and patted her mount who was becoming restless.

'It's absolutely exhilarating, but actually it's prohibited after eleven a.m. this time of the year.'

After their ride they got back in the car and stopped briefly at the village of Trinity where he pointed out the church with its spire that was 410 feet above sea level, before driving on to Bouley Bay where they visited the harbour café for refreshments.

She enjoyed the coffee and cakes but suddenly Justin's mood had changed for he seemed preoccupied — almost distant. She hoped he was not regretting having kissed her that morning. Perhaps he kissed all the girls he met and they weren't so foolish as to consider it as anything other than a compliment.

Presently he said, 'I'm afraid I've got to be away for a couple of days on Alderney. I could have done without it, but my client was most insistent that I go over in person. It would appear that telephones and fax machines aren't enough on this occasion.'

She felt irrationally disappointed but also relieved, as she realised that this must have been what was occupying his mind. Perhaps it was just as well, for it would give her some space to get herself together and analyse her feelings.

'But you will be back in time for the dinner party on Saturday, won't you?' she asked anxiously.

'Of course, and I'm only sorry that it's worked out this way, but when business calls there's not a lot I can do about it.'

They went down to the beach where cliffs almost 500 feet high towered above them. 'It's not the best of places for swimming,' he said, 'because the shore shelves into deep water, but it's a good spot for scuba diving and fishing and the pebbles are certainly worth a second glance.'

He put an arm lightly about her waist as they hunted for different coloured pebbles along the beach. She realised that she felt at ease with him and knew she was going to miss him whilst he was away.

On Friday, Amber and Bethany accompanied their father and Aunt Sophie on a shopping trip to St. Helier. They spent an interesting time at the Central Market which Sophie informed them had been built in 1882. They wandered amongst the colourful displays of flowers, fruit and vegetables housed under a glass canopy. Whilst Sophie purchased cheeses and freshly baked bread nearby, they amused themselves by watching the golden carp swimming in the pool beneath an ornate fountain.

Distributing her parcels amongst them, Sophie announced that it was time for coffee and marched them along the pedestrian precincts to her favourite pavement café. After a while, Peter got to his feet and offering to deposit the shopping back in the car where there was a cool box, said that he intended to spend the rest of the morning in the Bibliothèque Publique.

'Right — now we can get down to the real business of the day,' Sophie informed them and led the way to de Gruchy's department store.

'No trip to Jersey is complete without a visit here', she said. It soon became apparent why as they stopped to look at the fashions by internationally famous names or to have a spray of the fabulously expensive perfumes on offer.

'Well, I suppose there's no harm in imagining what it would be like to be able to afford to dress like this,' Amber murmured when they were out of earshot.

'Do you suppose Aunt Sophie actually shops here?'

'Oh yes, but don't go getting any ideas, Amber. We'll have to make do with the chain stores, unless I find myself a millionaire, of course!'

Even though they didn't buy much, they had to admit that it had been an experience that they wouldn't have missed. They were having lunch when an elegant, beautifully coiffured lady greeted Sophie from a nearby table and then came across to speak with them.

'My dear Harriet, how lovely to see you — I thought you and Giles were still away.' Sophie kissed the woman's proffered cheek.

'We got back the day before yesterday.' She looked curiously at Bethany and Amber.

'These are my nieces, Bethany and Amber Tyler — this is my dear friend Harriet Le Feuvre. Harriet, you and Giles must come to my dinner party tomorrow if you're free!'

'What fun — you haven't had a dinner party for ages. Of course we'll come, darling. Do I take it Justin will be there?'

'But of course.' Sophie gave her a knowing smile. 'He's away on Alderney at present, and Fenella will be coming over especially.'

Harriet Le Feuvre arched her beautifully shaped eyebrows. 'Oh, so they are still . . . I thought at one time . . . '

Amber could scarcely conceal her impatience with this irritating conversation and, once Harriet Le Leuvre had gone back to her own table, she turned to her aunt and asked, 'Who's Fenella? Is she Justin's girlfriend?'

A smile played about Sophie's lips. 'Fenella Moignard is another very dear friend of mine and I suppose — yes, she is Justin's lady friend.'

'And she's coming to your dinner party?' Amber pursued.

Sophie looked keenly at Bethany, almost as if to watch her reaction.

'I sincerely hope so, because she is someone I particularly want you both to meet.'

Although it was a warm day, Bethany suddenly felt chilled. She had kept hoping that perhaps her father had got it wrong — that there really wasn't anyone special in Justin's life and that his kisses had meant something, after all. Now, like a douche of cold water, she realised sadly that just like many other men, he enjoyed playing the field in order to boost his male ego. She supposed he must be having a good laugh at her expense.

'What is it, my dear? You've gone quite pale,' Sophie said and, just for an instant, Bethany imagined that her aunt could see into her mind and read her thoughts.

'Oh, I'm fine, Aunt Sophie — just a little tired, perhaps,' she assured her. Fenella Moignard was obviously the glamorous redhead her father had mentioned. They had not even met, but Bethany had a distinct feeling that they would not get along too well. She should have known better than to lose her heart to someone like Justin Rochel, but it was equally his fault for leading her on. He had the ability to make her feel wanted and beautiful and, right now, that was what she needed more than anything else.

On Saturday, Bethany managed to persuade Aunt Sophie to allow her to do some flower arrangements for the dinner party. Great armfuls of lilies and roses were brought to her by the gardener and she spent a wonderful time arranging them.

'You've got a real flair, Bethany,' Sophie said, admiring the apricot and cream arrangement in the dining room and the tiny matching posies for the table itself. 'Justin told me about your flower festival. These are quite charming . . . Now, come and tell me what you think of my desserts, my dear. I need an opinion.'

Sophie had surpassed herself and Bethany realised that, in quite a different way, her aunt was equally as creative as herself.

Bethany had bought a black evening dress on an impulse in the sale in Horsham, knowing that its classical style wouldn't date. It showed off her trim figure to its best advantage. For decoration she added a thick gold chain that had belonged to her mother and the pearl tear-drop earrings that she had used in her display for the flower festival. Amber had found time to do her sister's hair and help her with her make-up before being whisked off to James Vautier's party.

As Bethany made her way along the corridor Justin's door opened and he stood there preventing her from passing. He looked devastatingly handsome in his white tuxedo. His brown eyes swept over her appraisingly from her gleaming smoothly upswept hair to the high heeled black shoes until she wondered if there was something wrong with her appearance after all.

'Will I do?' she found herself asking foolishly.

For answer he took her hand and said, 'You've taken my breath away, Bethany Tyler! Can you really be the same rather serious young woman who served me in the bookshop? You look like an advertisement for a Paris fashion magazine.'

She was powerless to move. It was as if a magnetism exuded from him keeping her there against her will. She was standing so close that she could smell the warm spicy scent of the cologne he used and, suddenly, she wanted to reach up and touch his face, tracing the rugged features as if to memorise every detail. She could not know that he was controlling himself with the greatest difficulty, wondering what on earth it was about this girl that made him want to touch her every time he saw her. Abruptly he released her hand.

'You'll do fine,' he said, 'and now we'd better go downstairs before the guests begin to arrive.'

Peter Tyler was looking scholarly in one of Cedric Rochel's dinner jackets. Bethany stood by his side and, hopefully, did all that was expected of her. Large dinner parties like this were rather out of her league, she reflected. Sophie and Justin's friends were pleasant enough but seemed to be from another world. She was aware that they were part of Jersey's glittering social set — most of them extremely wealthy; some in the millionaire bracket. No wonder Sophie needed so much money if she insisted upon entertaining on this lavish scale.

Bethany looked in vain for someone to relate to who seemed just the tiniest bit ordinary. At length she decided that

Dr. Mauger and his wife and son Martin, seemed to be more on her wave-length. Presently, Martin glancing in her direction and seeing she was alone came across to talk with her. He was fair-haired with pleasant features and rather serious blue eyes.

'So you're the prodigal niece?'

'One of them . . . my sister's attending a sixteenth birthday party on a yacht . . . What sort of work do you do?'

'I'm a financial adviser.' He named the bank in St. Helier where he worked. 'So if you happen to have the odd couple of million floating about that you want to invest then I'm your man.'

She laughed. 'You've got to be joking — if only. Seriously, I wouldn't know what to do with a vast sum of money like that.'

He placed his empty wine glass on a nearby tray.

'Most of the folk in this room don't seem to have that problem. They get through money like there's no tomorrow — still if it wasn't for the likes of them I guess I'd be out of a job!'

'I suppose that's one way of putting it. The idle rich still provide a fair amount of work for the poorer people.'

'So you don't believe in a classless society either then?'

'I might believe in it, but the chances of it coming to fruition are virtually nil and so we might as well settle for what we've got.'

'True.' He looked about him. 'This place is quite something, isn't it?'

'Surely you've been here before?' she asked in some surprise.

He shook his head. 'As a matter of fact, no, although my parents have several times. I think Mrs. Le Claire invited me here this evening with the express purpose of introducing me to you. I bet we're sitting next to each other at dinner.'

She grinned. 'Come to think of it we are, but if you can't bear the thought, I could be very wicked and swap you over with my father.'

He laughed. 'What and risk the wrath of your aunt? Not likely.'

'Well then, we'll just have to make the best of the situation, won't we?' She wondered who Justin was sitting beside. There was a slight stir as some more guests arrived. Glancing towards the doorway, she saw Harriet Le Feuvre with a silver-haired, distinguished-looking gentleman, presumably her husband, Giles, and behind them a very beautiful woman with a mass of auburn hair wearing an amazing glittering green gown that showed off her splendid curvaceous figure.

'Well! Well!' Martin said. 'It's Fenella Moignard! So the Merry Widow's back on the scene, is she?'

Justin and Sophie had gone over to greet the late arrivals. The woman turned her face to Justin to be kissed and he responded laughingly.

'Same old Fenella,' Martin commented. 'Always likes to make a bit of an entrance and to be the centre of attention. I have to say she does look pretty stunning. What a dress!'

The dress had cut away sides and a deep, plunging neckline and it was small wonder, thought Bethany, that dressed in such a provocative manner, Fenella Moignard proved so attractive to men.

'Did you say widow?' she queried when she could trust herself to speak.

'Yes, she married Guy Moignard about three years ago. He was a friend of your aunt's and the Rochels' and old enough to be Fenella's father. He was, however, a millionaire and so now she is exceedingly rich. He died barely a year ago and so we haven't seen too much of her recently. Apparently she's been on Alderney.'

'Alderney!' echoed Bethany and suddenly everything was crystal clear. Even if the 'client' Justin had needed to see so urgently on Alderney had not been Fenella, it was pretty evident that he had managed to fit her into his busy schedule. Bethany told herself that she had been a fool to imagine that he could possibly care for her. She wanted to ask Martin what he knew about Justin's relationship with Fenella Moignard — to find out how long they had known each other, for instance, but thought better of it.

Sophie put an arm about Fenella's shoulders and brought her across to Bethany just then.

'Bethany, I want you to meet a very dear friend of mine — Fenella Moignard . . . Fenella this is my niece, Bethany Tyler — and Martin Mauger, whom, of course, you know already.'

Close to, Bethany could see that Fenella was rather older than she had seemed at first glance. Her face was cleverly made up and the mass of bright hair added to her youthful appearance. She proffered a beautifully manicured hand.

'So you're Bethany, Sophie has told me so much about you.'

Bethany murmured something which she hoped sounded polite, wondering exactly what Sophie could have said. To her relief, shortly afterwards they went into dinner.

The meal was excellent from the lobster

terrine to the layers of strawberry shortcake and cream. Sophie certainly knew all about the art of entertaining, but Bethany was aware that the money raised from Swallowfield could not possibly provide her aunt with the sort of income that she would need for this sort of lifestyle. And then she realised that, in all probability, Justin would have paid for everything that evening. After all, it was his house and so, Bethany supposed that most of the people sitting at the enormous dining room table were his friends too.

Bethany had to admit that she found Martin Mauger good company, even though his jokes were a little obvious and his stories of work rather boring to those without a knowledge of Jersey's financial scene. The laughter, however, came mostly from Justin's end of the table and, glancing in that direction, she could see that Fenella had the attention of every man near her. No other woman could possibly compete whilst she was around. Bethany realised that Martin was speaking to her and focussed her attention on him.

'I'm so sorry, Martin — what did you say?'

He laughed. 'I said Fenella knows how to get everyone eating out of her hand, doesn't she? What a bewitching female she is!'

'I suppose she's known Justin for a long time?' She was concentrating on her dessert, not wanting to give herself away.

Martin looked at her in some surprise. 'Don't you know? They used to be engaged and then there was some kind of row and they broke it off. The next we knew Fenella had married Guy Moignard — as if on the rebound — and then, two years later, he popped his clogs . . . '

Bethany stared at him as the words slowly registered.

'And now she's free again and a wealthy woman.'

He finished his wine. 'She wasn't exactly poor to start with. She's an adored only child of rich parents. No, it was almost as though she married Guy Moignard in a fit of pique, but now it seems as if she's got her claws into Justin again.'

'Do I take it that you don't approve?'

He bit into a strawberry. 'Who am I to approve or disapprove? Her type are so artificial that I can't be doing with them, probably because I was brought up to believe in a totally different set of values. I could wish she'd let me manage her finances though!'

Justin was looking intently at Fenella,

obviously poring over every word that she said. With a sinking heart, Bethany had to acknowledge that they made an extremely attractive couple.

The meal ended with coffee, petit fours and liqueurs and, afterwards, the couples spilled onto the terrace and out into the garden. It was a mild evening and the scents of roses and honeysuckle were intoxicating. Coloured lights had been rigged up amongst the trees giving them a fairytale appearance.

'You know you've told me very little about yourself,' Martin said as they wandered through the rose garden.

'There's not much to tell.'

'So you don't have anyone special in your life at present then?'

'I haven't had time for romantic entanglements recently,' she informed him. 'I've had to make do with the fictitious characters from the books that we sell, I'm afraid.'

He laughed at that. 'Listen, I've got a bit of time owing to me . . . I was wondering if you'd like to come out with me one day next week?'

'Martin that would be lovely,' she said sincerely.

'How much longer are you planning to stay here?'

'Oh, about another ten days at the very most.'

'Well then, we'll just have to make the most of it, won't we?'

He took her hand lightly and she realised that an uncomplicated holiday fling with no strings attached might be just what she needed at the present moment. As they passed the rose arbour she glanced across and a sudden gleam of green caught her attention. Before she could look away she saw Justin and Fenella locked in a tight embrace.

'She doesn't believe in wasting any time, does she?' Martin remarked when they were barely out of earshot. 'I wonder if she married poor Guy Moignard for love, or just for his money and to spite Justin Rochel . . . Mind you — I gather Rochel isn't exactly short of a Jersey pound or two himself!'

'I wouldn't know,' Bethany said. She was feeling slightly nauseous; saddened that Justin should have used her as a plaything for it was now quite obvious that his affections lay elsewhere. Well, she had just learnt a very sobering lesson — that her judgement where men were concerned was even poorer than she had thought. Suddenly it was important to her to try to salvage something from this holiday and to let Justin know that she was quite capable of having a good time without him being there to entertain her.

Some time after eleven, Amber arrived back at Lilyville with James Vautier. 'Hallo Bethany — we've had the most amazing time.'

Bethany introduced them to Martin Mauger. 'I suppose you've found Aunt Sophie? She particularly wanted you to meet her friends.'

'Yes, I know — we've been speaking to some of them already . . . Where's Justin?'

'He's a little occupied at the moment,' Martin said swiftly. 'Can I get you all some drinks?'

When he had gone into the house, Amber said, 'What's he talking about? What's Justin doing?'

'He's with his guests,' Bethany informed her, but at that moment, Justin appeared with Fenella and Amber ran towards him.

'I suppose that's his girlfriend,' James remarked. 'My grandparents reckon she's one of the richest women in the Channel Isles.'

'So I gather,' Bethany said, 'but money isn't everything, you know. It can't buy health or happiness.'

'No, I suppose you're right — I like your sister, Miss Tyler. I was a bit bored before she came and now things have improved. We're having such a fab time.'

'Good — just remember to look after her though, won't you? She's still only fifteen.'

He nodded. 'Sure will — I've already had that conversation with my grandfather, so don't you worry.'

Bethany, nevertheless, was rather worried for they were so young and Amber hadn't had a proper boyfriend before. She rejoined them shortly afterwards, just as Martin reappeared with the drinks.

'Did you see that woman's dress! It must have cost an absolute fortune, but it was so revealing.'

'Well if you've got the figure flaunt it,' James grinned and Amber stamped on his foot.

'Men! That's all you ever think about! Brains are important too, you know.'

'Yes, but if you happen to be blessed with both then you're fortunate.'

They subsided into fits of giggles and, after a while, Martin and Bethany left them to their teenage chatter and wandered back into the house. The guests began to drift off soon after midnight and Sophie declared that it had been one of her most successful dinner parties ever.

Amber came into Bethany's room as she was preparing for bed.

'Whoever was that dreadful woman Justin was with tonight?'

'You know who it was — Fenella Moignard.'

'Surely Justin can't be serious about her, can he?'

'Apparently so — they were engaged, at one time, so Martin was telling me and then, soon after they broke it off, she married an elderly millionaire who died about a year ago, leaving her a vast fortune — so now she's the merry widow.'

'So why does she have to go back to Justin? I wonder who broke off the engagement?'

Bethany had been wondering that herself, but decided that it really wasn't important, because it was so obvious that they were back together again now.

'Well, I wouldn't stand for it, if I were you, Beth. I'd have it out with him.'

Bethany stared at her sister. 'Amber, whatever are you talking about?'

Amber tossed back her curls. 'The trouble with you, Bethany Tyler is that you just can't get it into your head that I'm grown up now. You will carry on treating me like a child. I'm practically sixteen, in case you'd forgotten, nearly old enough to get married myself. You and Justin have been going out together, haven't you? Don't deny it! . . . And now this woman's turned up and . . . '

'Amber, it's very late and I really don't want to discuss it. Fenella was Justin's lady friend way before I came on the scene, remember. He's just been friendly towards me, that's all . . . You've obviously been reading too much into the situation. You might like to know that I'm going out with Martin Mauger sometime next week. He's going to give me a ring . . . So, you see, you needn't worry about me.'

Bethany realised with a start that Amber did look decidedly grown-up that evening in the new white dress purchased in St. Helier. She had done her blonde hair in a more sophisticated style and her pretty face was lightly made-up.

'Martin seemed okay, but he's not in the same league as Justin — no way! Still if you want to let that Moignard woman whisk him away from beneath your very nose then that's up to you.'

'Yes,' Bethany said firmly. 'It most certainly is — so goodnight, Amber.'

When Bethany eventually fell asleep, she dreamt that Justin took her to one of the secluded beaches and left her there alone.

The tide was coming in, but she couldn't climb back up the cliff path, however hard she tried, and Fenella and Justin were standing watching her from the top and laughing.

7

Bethany awoke the next morning feeling as if she hadn't had any sleep at all. She crept into the kitchen and made herself a cup of tea and then, donning her swimming costume, pulled on a wrap-around skirt, grabbed a towel and set off for the pool. She couldn't believe it when she found Justin there before her.

'Come on in, it's just the thing to wake you up,' he greeted her.

Her first impulse was to leave him to it, but then she removed her wrap and slid into the water, gasping as its coldness hit her and struck out with strong strokes. After two lengths she pulled up beside him.

'Well, good morning, Bethany, and how are you?'

'Fine thanks,' she said briefly and was off again to the other side of the pool. Presently, she was aware that he had come to join her, surfacing beside her.

'Did you enjoy last evening?'

'Yes, and you most certainly did — so I don't need to ask you?'

He looked at her keenly and she was aware of his tanned muscular body gleaming with

158

droplets of water and her heart began to race uncontrollably. If he touched her now — if he made any move towards her whatsoever, then her newly made resolutions would go to the wind. It was quite useless for her to deny her attraction towards this man.

'Bethany, I'm sorry if you felt neglected last night, but as host, I had to do my duty to my other guests.'

'Oh, is that what you called it?' She met his gaze defiantly — Vandyke brown eyes and stormy grey ones locking together and then before she knew it, she was in his arms and his lips were seeking hers hungrily. She was aware of his muscular body moulding into hers, of a delicious feeling as she leant against his honeyed skin and their legs twined together beneath the water. Her arms slid about his neck, her fingers tangling in his thick hair. The sheer maleness of him set her aflame with desire. His lips moved over her bare shoulders and to the curves of her breasts.

'Well, that was quite some good morning, Miss Tyler,' he said at length. 'Have you really missed me that much?'

And she coloured, feeling that most probably he believed she had thrown herself at him. For answer she swam beneath the water and ended up on the opposite side of the pool only to find, when she surfaced, that he was waiting for her. She had regained her composure now and was annoyed that she had responded to him in the way that she had. The sound of someone calling to him broke the silence. Glancing up she saw Fenella Moignard looking incredible in a white sundress and waving a towel.

'The Caudeys' pool needs relining so Sophie said it would be all right to come over for a swim. I guessed you'd be here this time in the morning.'

'Yes, here we are,' Justin said, and just for a split second, Bethany thought she detected a slight note of impatience. Fenella stripped off the sundress and threw it casually over a lounger. She was wearing a minuscule white bikini in some shimmering material that displayed her well-endowed figure superbly. She dived in and then indulged in the kind of horseplay with Justin that was designed to make Bethany leave, but she stayed where she was amazed by the other woman's brazen behaviour.

After a bit, Fenella came to sit on the edge of the pool and Bethany saw that the bikini, now it was wet, was clinging to her like a second skin and was practically diaphanous.

'Darling,' Fenella said, tossing back her mane of red hair and looking critically at Bethany, 'what an incredibly sensible costume. You really ought to wear something a little more flattering to your figure.'

Bethany bit back a sharp retort, wondering if Justin had heard the remark. She climbed out of the pool, found her wrap and, draping the towel about her shoulders, called, 'Goodbye,' and made her way towards the house. When she looked back they were racing each other across the pool. She wondered if Justin had even noticed she had gone. Before long he would probably be making passionate love to Fenella, although Bethany could hardly blame him when the woman was virtually throwing herself at him in that outrageous garment that served as a bikini.

For a wild moment, Bethany wondered what effect it would have on Justin if she turned up wearing such a daring outfit, but she doubted if she could carry it off with the necessary panache. Why was she so unlucky in her choice of men, she wondered yet again. With a heavy heart, tears prickling her eyelids she went inside.

After a hasty breakfast she went to church with Amber and her father. When they returned, Justin and Fenella were sitting on the terrace with tall glasses of exotic-looking drinks in front of them.

'Oh, there you are!' Fenella said lazily. 'Sophie tells me you've been to church. How quaint — I didn't realise people actually went there any more, apart from going to funerals and weddings, of course.'

'Really? Well Justin does when he's in Applebourne,' Amber informed her.

Fenella shot an amused glance in Justin's direction. 'Oh? Well, I daresay there isn't too much else to do in such a sleepy little village, is there J.C.?'

'On the contrary, you would be surprised ... Ah, here's Sophie with coffee.' He got up and took the tray from her.

Fenella turned to Bethany. 'And what do you do in Sussex, Bethany?'

'My father owns a bookshop and I help him run it.'

'Indeed — don't you find that a little dull — surrounded by dusty old tomes?'

'Not at all,' Bethany said sweetly, 'I enjoy my work. I'm lucky to be in employment with so many out of work these days.'

Fenella shrugged. 'Oh well, each to his own, I suppose ... Did I tell you I'm doing a little work now and again, J.C.? Just to keep my hand in. In fact, I'm going to look up some old contacts tomorrow.'

Bethany was frankly amazed. She hadn't imagined that Fenella would do any work.

'What do you do?' She asked her curiously.

'I'm a consultant for beauty products ... I'll give you a special price for a consultation, if you like.' She fished in her handbag and brought out a card.

'Thank you, I'll bear it in mind,' Bethany said rather taken aback.

To Bethany's surprise, Fenella declined Sophie's invitation to stay on for lunch.

'Much as I'd love to, I must spend some time with the Caudeys'. It was so sweet of Henrietta and Piers to put me up . . . Such a busy household — four children, an au pair and two dogs.' She grimaced.

'Sounds fun,' Amber told her. 'Don't you like children?'

'Fenella prefers them when they're more grown up, don't you, my dear?' Sophie smiled and suddenly, Bethany wondered if this had been the reason for the broken engagement. Perhaps Fenella hadn't wanted children and Justin had. And then she told herself sternly not to speculate. Shortly afterwards Fenella departed and she felt a sense of relief.

They were in the middle of lunch when Mrs. Vibert appeared in the doorway and told Bethany that she was wanted on the 'phone. It was Martin Mauger to ask whether she thought Tuesday would be a good day

163

for them to go out, if he could arrange to get the time off work, and would she like to go to Samarès Manor? She told him, 'yes,' on both counts and returned to the table feeling pleased. Only the previous evening she had been in two minds whether to stay on for the remainder of the holiday or make some excuse to return to Applebourne early, but now it seemed as though things might improve. After all, she might as well enjoy herself whilst she had the opportunity.

After lunch Peter and Sophie announced that they were going to watch a programme on T.V. and Amber said that she was going to sunbathe by the pool. Bethany was about to follow them from the room when Justin waylaid her.

'That just leaves you and I, Bethany, so how about coming for a walk?'

'I was planning to do some painting this afternoon,' she said rather stiffly.

'You can always do that tomorrow when I'm working . . . Bethany, have I done something to annoy you?'

'No,' she answered unsteadily, unable to meet his gaze. Why couldn't she bring herself to tell him that she didn't want him to play fast and loose with her emotions — to use her for his amusement and then cast her off as soon as Fenella came on the scene? He put his hand under her chin, forcing her to look at him.

'Was it because of this morning? Perhaps I felt you wanted me to make love to you when you didn't, is that it? I thought you were sending out vibes, but I've obviously misinterpreted you.'

This was so far removed from the truth that she could not trust herself to answer him.

'I'm feeling rather tired, that's all,' she said and breaking away from him, collected her paints and went into the summer house. It was always the same, she reflected. Whenever she became involved with anyone, another woman turned up on the scene. This was like a repeat performance of her previous experience with Toby and Dianne. The secret was to keep herself busy, she told herself. Tomorrow she would see if there was anything she could do to help Aunt Sophie. She turned to her painting and was still engrossed in her work when Amber came to find her.

'Oh, what are you doing now? Let me see . . . That's really very good. Beth, would you mind very much if I didn't go for that walk with you tomorrow, after all?'

Bethany set down her brushes. 'Another day with James and Charlotte?'

'Just James, actually — he rang a few minutes ago. Charlotte and Mrs. Vautier are going shopping so we thought we'd hire some cycles.'

'Aren't you seeing rather a lot of James?'

Amber tossed back her curls. 'What if I am? There's no harm in it.'

'Just don't get too involved, love . . . We're returning to Swallowfield in just over another week's time and I've no idea when we'll be back.'

Amber scowled at her sister. 'You know I heard Fenella telling Justin she thought you were old-fashioned and I guess she's right . . . This holiday's been fab and if I hadn't come, I wouldn't have met James and no-one is going to separate us.'

Bethany snapped her paintbox shut and went to wash her brushes. She might have expected Fenella to have made some remark about her, but it still stung. Was she really that out of touch with the real world? Just lately she couldn't even seem to relate to her own sister. She found her father in the sitting-room reading the Sunday papers.

'Hallo Beth, what's wrong? You're looking a bit put out.'

She sank into a seat beside him. 'Dad, I think Amber is getting rather romantic notions about James Vautier. She's at a

166

vulnerable age and she's not had much experience of boys — I'm just a bit afraid she might lose her head.'

Her father laughed. 'Is that what's bothering you? She's sensible enough and, besides, the Vautiers seem nice people. I don't think we need worry on that score.'

Bethany firmly removed his newspaper. 'Dad, the days of the chaperone have long since gone. Amber's just told me she and James are going off cycling together tomorrow.'

Her father raised his eyebrows. 'I'll have a quiet word with her. It'll be all right. She's entitled to some fun, after all.'

And Bethany had to be contented with that. The following morning Justin drove Amber to meet up with the Vautiers on his way to St. Helier. The bike ride had been approved, but there were conditions.

Bethany encountered Mrs. Vibert coming from Aunt Sophie's room with a practically untouched breakfast tray.

'Mrs. Le Claire isn't feeling too well this morning — a bad headache,' the older woman said by way of explanation.

'Thank you for telling me, Mrs. Vibert. I'll see if there's anything I can do.' Bethany knocked briefly and went inside.

Aunt Sophie was lying slumped against

167

the pillows looking decidedly wan, her long hair spread about her. Without make-up she appeared distinctly unwell.

'I'm sorry to hear you're feeling ill, Aunt Sophie — is there anything I can do for you?'

Sophie reached for Bethany's hand and patted it. 'No — no, there's probably nothing anyone can do, Bethany. I'll know for certain when I've seen the consultant.'

Bethany sat down on the chair by the side of the bed.

'Consultant? I'm sorry, Aunt Sophie, but I don't understand. I thought you had a headache.'

She nodded. 'I do, but it's probably just the worry of it all. Your father and Justin obviously thought it best not to say anything to you and Amber for the moment . . . You see, I might have to have an operation. They think there's a tumour but they can't or won't say any more.'

Sophie looked so scared that Bethany's heart went out to her. She thought of her own mother and how ill she had been and then she said quickly. 'I'm sure it'll be all right, Aunt Sophie — try not to worry.'

A tear squeezed from Sophie's eye and she blinked it away impatiently. 'I've felt so wretched lately and for ages they couldn't

seem to find out what's wrong and now . . . '
She pointed to her abdomen. 'That was the
reason I needed to see you all — just in
case. I wanted to make it right with my
family. I know it's what my mother would
have wanted.'

'Oh, Aunt Sophie and we're glad you did,
but you mustn't look on the black side, you
know . . . When have you got to go to the
hospital?'

'This afternoon. Your father's taking
me — he's been wonderful, a tower of
strength . . . I do so want us all to be
friends.'

'Well, we are,' Bethany soothed her,
wishing her father had said something
about Sophie's illness. 'You know, I have
a feeling there might be things I can do for
you . . . You see, I prefer to be busy.'

Sophie smiled. 'You're so like me — that's
what's been so dreadful about the way I've
been feeling. I haven't been able to do all the
things I like to do, but dear Fenella is going
to come and give me a facial this morning
before she returns to Alderney, and then I'm
sure I'll feel much more like my old self. I do
so fret about Justin being on his own . . . I
just hope now that Fenella is free again and
they are both a bit older, they will find
happiness with each other. I would so like

to see them settled before — before.'

There was nothing Bethany could say to that. After a bit she ran her aunt a bath, poured in some lavender oil and left her in a much calmer state than when she had found her.

Peter Tyler was in the study browsing through the book-lined shelves. He looked up smilingly as his daughter entered the room.

'Hallo Beth, Sophie has asked me if I'd like to catalogue her books so I thought I'd make a start this morning. What are you planning to do with yourself today?'

She ignored his question and came straight to the point.

'Dad, whyever didn't you tell me that Aunt Sophie is ill?'

Her father blinked, 'Oh, so she's told you, has she? Justin and I thought it better not to say anything for the present. Well, darling I'm sure there's nothing to worry about. Anyway, we'll have a clearer idea of what's wrong when she sees the consultant again this afternoon. He's going to decide whether or not she needs an operation.'

That was her father all over, pushing away the unpleasant things in life and being the perpetual optimist. He was apt to pretend that problems simply didn't exist. 'Would you like me to come with you, this afternoon — just in case?'

'Oh, no, you've had to cope with enough illness in recent years . . . I tell you what though, let's meet up for tea afterwards to take her mind off things and then, if she feels like it, perhaps we can go for a little drive.'

The afternoon passed pleasantly enough for Bethany. Peter Tyler had dropped her off in St. Aubin and she wandered round the delightful fishing village looking in the shops and ships chandlers and eventually wending her way down to the harbour where she admired the granite houses built in the days when this had been a lively port and the centre for Jersey's cod fishing industry. She stood watching the fishing boats which made a colourful scene.

She was due to meet up with Aunt Sophie and her father at three thirty and was just wandering back along a cobbled street when someone hooted at her from a car. She spun round and found Martin Mauger grinning at her.

'Hi, you've saved me a phone call. It's okay for tomorrow. I'll pick you up around 9.30, shall I?'

They chatted for a few moments and then he said, 'Regretfully, I've got to go. I'm meeting a client in ten minutes.'

She waved goodbye and set off to find the teashop where she had arranged to meet her father and Sophie. They were a few minutes late and Bethany was beginning to feel a little anxious.

Over tea and scones at which Sophie only picked, they said very little. At length Bethany broached the subject which was uppermost in all their minds. 'So what's your news, Aunt Sophie?'

Her aunt sighed. 'An operation, I'm afraid, my dear, in about a week's time . . . They can't or won't say whether there's any cause for alarm. You know what these medical people are like. Dr. Mauger is a dear, so reassuring and the consultant's the same but, at the end of the day, I need to know the truth.'

Peter patted her arm. 'I'm sure you'll be fine, Sophie, so just you relax.'

'I could wish,' she said in between sips of tea, 'that you weren't planning to return to England just as I'm going into hospital. It would be such a comfort to know that you were around — especially if — if . . . 'Her eyes brimmed with tears and she blew her nose.

'Now don't you worry, Sophie. We won't desert you just when you need us most,' Peter assured her.

Bethany shot him a glance, as her aunt composed herself, whipping out a compact and dabbing powder on her nose. He winked at his daughter in a way which she knew meant he would talk about it later. It was all very well making promises but, much as she wouldn't want to leave her aunt, there was the bookshop and Swallowfield to consider. Perhaps she ought to offer to go back to England so that her father could stay on here. Suddenly she wished she could speak with Justin; he was always so rational.

The sky clouded over and there was a sudden downpour of rain at that point which knocked the idea of a drive on the head. It had been rather a sombre tea-party and Bethany, who had a kind heart, wished she could think of something to cheer her aunt up. It was her father who suggested that, before returning to Lilyville, they might take a look at the antique shop in which Justin had a part share. Bethany was intrigued for it was news to her that Justin still partly owned the business.

Aunt Sophie perked up considerably as they approached the shop on the outskirts of St. Helier and they spent a pleasant half hour browsing amongst the bric à brac and gleaming furniture.

'I haven't seen you for a while, Mrs. Le Claire,' Justin's partner commented.

'No, well I've decided that it's high time I called halt. I've enough china and silverware for three houses, I should think. You know I can't resist pretty things, Andrew.' She stopped in front of a display of silver tea-spoons. 'These are absolutely charming . . . I'll have this one and — yes, that.' He wrapped them up for her and she said:

'Who knows, next time I might be selling you something. After all, some of what I've purchased over the years was intended for investment purposes.'

'Does Justin still take an interest in the shop?' Bethany found herself asking, as they headed back to Lilyville.

'Oh yes — but, of course, he doesn't get a great deal of time nowadays so he treats it as a hobby. If he had decided to purchase your furniture it would probably have ended up there — but he obviously thought it looked a great deal better where it was.'

'Yes,' Bethany was thoughtful. It seemed as if there was no end to Justin's enterprises. A part-share in the shop would mean a part-share in the profits. It appeared that Justin, besides being an astute business man, was also more wealthy than she could ever have imagined. She couldn't help thinking, however, that if her father had been prepared to sell his collection of first editions in order to raise essential funds then, perhaps Sophie ought to have done likewise and sold some of her collection of silver and china as a token gesture.

She was, however, very touched when, at dinner, her aunt presented her and Amber with the Victorian tea-spoons.

Later Bethany went to have a quiet word with her father. She found him in the study. 'Dad, I don't like making promises we can't keep.'

He was thumbing through some copies of Anthony Trollope. 'Very nice editions these . . . What's that about promises, Beth?'

'You know we've arranged to return to England next week, so why tell Aunt Sophie we'll be around when she has her operation?'

Peter Tyler looked thoughtful. 'Hmn — I've been meaning to talk to you about that, darling, . . . Would you mind very much if we stayed on for a bit longer? Just until we see how she's going on? I'm sure John Lawrence is managing perfectly well — in fact, when I spoke with him on the phone yesterday, he seemed to be enjoying himself. I know Sophie has lots of friends, but it's not the same as having your family around you, at a time like this, is it? D'you know that

175

one of the reasons she wanted to meet us was because she wanted to put things right between us, just in case anything happened, and she didn't get the chance . . . I happen to know she's absolutely terrified of this operation. Never been in hospital before, you see, and dreading the anaesthetic. We really ought to be there, darling, to give her moral support, wouldn't you agree?'

For answer Bethany hugged her father. 'Oh Dad, you really are the kindest man. Of course we'll stay on for a little while longer. After all, one of us can always pop over to England for a couple of days or so, in between if need be. It isn't that far away.'

Amber was overjoyed at the prospect of an extended holiday, but managed to sober down when she learnt about Sophie's illness.

'Why do all the nice people get ill? First Grandpa and then Mummy and our Grandmother, and now Aunt Sophie. Life does seem so unfair sometimes.'

'I know, Amber, but try not to let Aunt Sophie see how upset you are. She needs all the support she can get at this time. Hopefully, in about a week, it'll all be over and there will be nothing to worry about.'

'Do you suppose that's why she wanted us to come here so that she could reunite herself with her family before she dies?'

'She's not going to die — not yet, at any rate, darling,' Bethany said, giving her sister a hug and hoping that this were true.

Justin had driven Fenella to the airport and then gone on to have dinner with friends. She realised how much she missed him when he wasn't around. The knowledge that she would see more of him if she stayed on at Lilyville was bittersweet.

She encountered Justin at breakfast the next morning.

'It looks like the weather's behaving itself again after that unseasonal outburst yesterday afternoon,' he remarked. 'I've got to work until about fourish, but I've booked us on a ride for four thirty.'

'Then I'm afraid you've been a bit precipitate,' she informed him, 'because I'm going out with Martin Mauger and I really can't say what time I'll be back.'

His eyes narrowed. 'Martin Mauger — I wouldn't have thought he was your type.'

She was tempted to retort that she wouldn't have thought Fenella Moignard was his type either, but she bit it back realising how petty and childish it would have sounded.

'Oh well, I'll see what Amber's doing . . . Another time perhaps?'

She nodded. He could not know the bitter wave of disppointment that washed over her — that she would gladly have relinquished her outing with Martin in order to go riding with him, but then she told herself firmly that it was for the best. Besides, he had to learn that he couldn't just go making arrangements without consulting with her first.

She was undecided what to wear for her outing with Martin and, in the end, she chose a new denim skirt with a white cheesecloth blouse, and caught her hair back with one of Amber's velvet scrunchies.

Martin Mauger turned up promptly at nine thirty looking rather different from the previous times Bethany had seen him, dressed in jeans and a Jersey sweater.

'You're looking good,' he said as he opened the car door for her.

Samarès Manor set in fourteen acres of beautiful gardens met up to Bethany's expectations. They took a tour of the estate in a horse-drawn van and Bethany learnt that the original manor house dated back to the middle ages and had always played an important part in Jersey life.

'At one time only the lords of the manors were permitted to keep pigeons,' Martin informed her, as they paused to look at the early eleventh century colombier or devecot that looked like a round ivy-clad tower.

Later as they sat over an enjoyable lunch

in the restaurant, Bethany told Martin that she would be staying on at Lilyville for a little longer whilst her aunt was in hospital.

'Well, I'm naturally sorry to hear of your aunt's illness, but I have to say how pleased I am that we'll have the chance of seeing a bit more of each other . . . So how come you haven't been to Jersey before?'

She set down her knife and fork. 'It's a long story — I'll give you a potted version, shall I?'

He listened intently and then said, 'It sounds like something out of a novel, and all this time haven't you wondered what it was like at Lilyville?'

'Well, of course, but I adored my grandfather and felt that my grandmother had been rather unfair towards him — walking out like that. I suppose they were just too young when they got married and, I can understand how my grandmother must have missed Jersey. I have to admit that my grandfather could be rather stubborn at times and dig his heels in. Katherine was homesick and not very strong, and apparently she simply could not settle in England . . . Perhaps if my grandfather had been more sympathetic . . . but that's all water under the bridge now. Anyway, I'm here now and I like my Aunt Sophie.'

'And Justin Rochel — what do you make of him?'

Bethany swallowed. 'He's very kind to Aunt Sophie, and he is our host and has made us very welcome.'

'Mmn, but it all seems so odd — your grandmother leaving all her money and Lilyville to Cedric Rochel . . . I'm surprised Mrs. Le Claire didn't contest the will.'

'Oh, but she was well catered for and now that Justin owns Lilyville he'll continue to look after her.'

Martin shook his head. 'Well, if you'll pardon my saying so it's still an odd set-up . . . Don't you wonder what will happen if he gets married?'

Of course she wondered that and, if it were to that dreadful Fenella Moignard — then what if she chose to come and live at Swallowfield? And then she grinned for, however much she would hate it, she could not help thinking about the effect Fenella would have on some of Applebourne's village folk.

'What's so funny?' he demanded.

'Oh, just an amusing thought.' She had no intention of telling him about Justin putting up the money for Sophie's share of Swallowfield — not yet at any rate. She wiped her mouth on her napkin. 'That was perfectly delicious, Martin . . . Are we going to see the rest of this place now?'

They had a guided tour of the house, admiring the fine walnut panelled dining-room and the drawing-room in William and Mary style. Afterwards they wandered round the herb garden.

'This is one of the largest herb gardens in Britain,' Martin told her as she bent to sniff some rosemary.

Finally they visited the Herb Shop at the front gate.

'Oh what a wonderful smell,' she said, inhaling the fragrances of herbs and pot-pourri. She bought some lavender soap for Aunt Sophie to take with her into hospital and Martin purchased a souvenir book about the Manor. Altogether it had been a thoroughly enjoyable visit.

Before taking her home Martin drove her to St. Clement's church where they paused to look at the frescoes which had only been discovered beneath the plaster in 1879. Their last port of call was to see the Victor Hugo Hotel.

'This is where Victor Hugo lived and wrote before he was banished in 1855. No. 3 Marina Terrace is now part of the hotel and they'll show you the poet's room on request.'

181

When they arrived back at Lilyville he leant across and gave her a chaste kiss on the cheek.

'I hope you'll come out with me again. I've enjoyed your company', he said and she felt a little as if she had been his maiden aunt. She thanked him and realised how pleasant it was to have such an undemanding relationship.

She located her father in the sitting-room. He looked up from the book he was reading with a smile. 'Hallo Beth — did you have a good day?' And then, without waiting for her reply, he continued, 'Darling, I've just spoken with John Lawrence about carrying on full-time at the shop . . . '

'And — is he all right about it?'

'Ye-es.' But there was something about her father's expression that told her this wasn't quite accurate. 'So what's troubling you?'

'You don't miss a trick, do you Beth? Well, it's just that . . . Oh, I'm sure there's nothing for us to be concerned about but Lily, bless her heart, it was just the way she said, 'We'll be so glad to see you and Miss Tyler back — things are a bit busy here.' And then, when I talked to John, I gathered that he's been finding it all a bit more hectic than he'd previously admitted. Nevertheless, he's prepared to soldier on for a bit, but he's reminded me that I've promised to honour his holiday later on this month.'

'Well, surely we'll be back by then, Dad, and, if not, then I'll go and hold the fort.'

He dropped a kiss on her forehead. 'What would we do without you, Beth? I've realised just recently just how much we've put upon you during these past few years. You've never complained when I've beem away, even though it's meant cutting into your precious free time.'

'Nonsense, you know I've wanted to keep busy since Toby — since . . . Anyway, that's a thing of the past. You'll be pleased to know that he's finally out of my system.'

'I am — and it's good that you've found Martin to go out with. He seems a nice young man.'

'Now don't you go jumping to any conclusions, Dad. Martin took me out to show me the Jersey sights — that's all. He probably won't even ask me out again. After all, there isn't a great deal of point, is there, when he's here in Jersey and I'm living in England.'

'But, if he did ask you, would you go?' her father persisted.

She considered this. 'Probably — he's nice,

uncomplicated company and couldn't I do with that just now!'

It was apparent that Justin, coming into the sitting-room just then, had heard that last remark and Bethany, seeing his expression, wished she could have retracted it.

8

The following morning, Sophie asked Bethany if she would like to take a look in the attics as there were some things that might interest her, including the diaries that Justin had mentioned.

The attics at Lilyville were extensive and obviously very rarely visited. Bethany was in her element as Sophie unearthed various leather-bound photograph albums and a couple of boxes full of keepsakes, including one or two items that had originally belonged to Grandpa Tyler. There were christening presents, napkin rings and her grandmother's wedding dress.

'There's such a lot I still don't understand, Aunt Sophie. My father doesn't want to talk about what happened and I realise it must have been painful for you both.'

'It was — but I just think it was one of those things. Your grandfather met my mother during the war, as I'm sure you know. Katherine had been sent to stay with a cousin in England the moment the threat of an invasion hung over Jersey. It was a typical wartime romance. They were very young and very much in love to begin with, and then I'm afraid the inevitable happened — my mother found she was expecting Peter and so, as soon as he got some leave, they married. Unfortunately, she could never adapt to a life in England and, once my father returned from the war, he was not prepared to leave Applebourne and Swallowfield again to go to Jersey. He would not even meet his wife half-way and go for a visit.'

'I'm sure my mother tried to make her marriage work, but it was hard for her because, in those days, your great grandmother was still alive and very much the mistress at Swallowfield. Katherine felt overshadowed by her and then, of course, it was a hard time and there was never too much money to spare. Anyway, one day your grandparents had a very strong disagreement and it was then that Katherine decided my father would have to choose between Swallowfield and herself. He could not bring himself to leave Applebourne and his mother and so Katherine returned to Lilyville bringing me with her. She once told me that it had been the hardest decision of her life and that, even then, she thought my father would change his mind and come after her. Peter was always your grandfather's favourite and so, I suppose that was why my mother took me with her, and I have to say that I never really missed Swallowfield, after the first few weeks, because I was made so welcome here.'

It had been fascinating for Bethany to hear Sophie's version of the story which she had pieced together from her father over the years from the tiny fragments he had been prepared to tell her. Besides the diaries, one of the boxes contained a pile of neatly folded letters tied with a piece of faded blue ribbon.

'These make interesting reading. They're early letters to your grandfather from Katherine from the time she came back to Lilyville.'

'He returned them?' Bethany asked in disbelief.

Sophie nodded. 'It was as if he swept out every memory of my mother and myself. I found it hard to forgive him for that. He probably loved Katherine so deeply that he simply could not believe that she would desert him. Cedric Rochel was a lodger at Lilyville and, gradually, my mother and he fell in love and . . . Well, you know the rest. Anyway, let's go and get some coffee now. You may keep the letters if they interest you and the diaries too. If you want to take them back with you to England then please do so.

They'll only stay up here otherwise.'

'Have you ever read them, Aunt Sophie?' Sophie hesitated.

'I have glanced at them, yes. We didn't come across them until recently. I think your grandmother must have put them up here just before she died or maybe Cedric found them amongst her possessions and decided this was the best place for them. Anyway, it's up to you what you do with them now.'

Bethany felt rather sad at the thought of what had happened. If she had children then, no matter what the circumstances, she would make certain that they knew both their parents.

They went downstairs and took the photograph albums out onto the terrace where they spent a happy time looking through them together.

As Bethany flipped over the pages of black and white photographs set in beautiful frames decorated with painted flowers, she came across some later ones in colour and, studying them, gasped in surprise.

'But those are of my parents . . . and you're in the photographs too! Aunt Sophie, I hadn't realised that you had met my mother!'

'Oh yes, my dear on several occasions. She never came to Lilyville — we always met on one of the other islands. Peter did not mention it to your grandfather because, so far as he was concerned, his wife and daughter had ceased to exist years back. As time went on, I came to consider Cedric as my father, but I could never forget Peter and when I got married I sent him an invitation to my wedding. He didn't accept but he did keep in touch, after that, and your grandfather knew that much. Peter married shortly afterwards and we decided that we'd all meet up on Guernsey and so that's what we did.'

Bethany was frankly amazed. 'I don't know why Dad didn't tell me all this — and did you ever see my grandfather again?'

Sophie shook her head sorrowfully. 'No — I refused to go to England, you see, but your grandmother did. She went to the hospital and sat with him just before he died and I did send him a letter which I know she read to him — and a photograph. No-one could have been more surprised than myself when I discovered he had left me a part share in Swallowfield in his will.'

There was a long pause and then Sophie said, 'Family feuds are a big mistake, Bethany. Life is too short to be bitter which is why I so wanted your father to bring you both over here before it was too late.'

'And we're very glad we came, Aunt

189

Sophie,' Bethany assured here, 'but I do
so wish you'd come to Swallowfield when
you're better.'

'I don't think so, Bethany . . . but I'm
pleased that Justin is putting up the money
so that you can remain there. I have to admit
there was a part of me that was glad when I
thought it had to be sold and, I know that
was very selfish but I've grown to care for
my brother and I wanted all those unhappy
early memories to be washed away.'

'Then we won't talk about them any more
if you don't want to, but I'm really pleased
to know that you met my mother.'

'Elizabeth was a delightful lady and it was
so sad that her life was cut off at such an
early age. I know your father and her were
sublimely happy.' Sophie got to her feet. 'I
just need to have a word with Mrs. Vibert.'

Bethany took the letters and diaries up to
her room and placed them carefully in one
of the drawers and then she went in search of
her father who was immersed in cataloguing
Sophie's library.

'Dad, why didn't you tell me that you and
Mum used to meet up with Aunt Sophie and
her husband?' she demanded.

He looked taken aback. 'Oh, Sophie told
you, did she? Well, it was a long time ago
when we were first married, darling. It didn'

occur to me that it would be that important to you to know about it.'

'So you haven't seen each other in recent years then?' she persisted.

He replaced a couple of books on the shelf. 'Yes, as a matter of fact we saw her again about a year before your mother died. I thought a holiday might do her good and Sophie suggested we went to Sark and we met up with her there . . . '

'But you didn't mention it.' Bethany started at him accusingly.

'Oh, you must have known about the holiday but you were away at university and Amber was at boarding school.'

Bethany felt certain that there were still things which he had not told her, but there had been so many revelations that morning that she felt unable to cope with any more right now.

Before lunch she slipped into the garden. It was such a quiet haven with its colourful borders and wonderful fragrances. Turning a corner she practically cannoned into Justin. He steadied her and immediately her heart began to pound. It was as if she could feel the vibes coming from him.

'Oh, I'm so sorry, Justin,' she gasped. He held her fractionally longer than was necessary and she noticed the fresh smell

191

of his cologne — a different one today, obviously to match his mood. His dark eyes locked with hers.

'Your father and I are going to an auction this afternoon — there might be some books . . . D'you want to come along too?'

'Yes please, I'd like that,' she said without hesitation. She moved away from him wanting to gain control, hoping he had no idea of the effect he had on her. This was ridiculous! She really must pull herself together. Just then Amber came rushing out of the house.

'Aunt Sophie said to tell you lunch is ready — oh, and the hospital has just rung to tell her she needs to be there next Tuesday morning.'

'Right — then I suggest that between now and Sophie going into hospital we have a thoroughly enjoyable time,' Justin said.

Bethany found the auction interesting. Her father bought four books. 'For the shop,' he told Bethany, but she suspected he might be starting up his collection again. Justin purchased a number of small items which he apparently intended to put in his rooms at Swallowfield and one or two larger pieces of furniture for the antique business.

Martin Mauger rang soon after they arrived back at Lilyville, wanting to know if Bethany was free to go out to dinner with him that evening. Apparently, there was a seafood restaurant he was keen to take her to. She told him she would love to go and took a lot of care over her appearance. She chose to wear a bright pink sleeveless dress and matching jacket with black leather sandals, and swept her long hair up on top of her head. She added a pair of dangling jet earrings and put on rather more make-up than usual.

She passed Justin on her way downstairs and he gave her an appraising glance. 'So where are you off to?'

'Your guess is as good as mine,' she told him airily. 'Martin is taking me out to dinner, but I don't know the venue . . . It's a surprise.'

'Well, enjoy yourself,' he said, as if he couldn't really have cared less, and went off in the direction of his office.

Bethany could have wished that he had at least indicated by his manner that he was sorry she was spending the evening with someone else. She could not even tell if he approved of what she was wearing, even though it was an outfit he hadn't seen her in before. Well what did it matter what he thought? she asked herself crossly. She was determined to have a good time in spite of Justin Rochel.

'Whow!' Martin whistled appreciatively when she opened the door.

'You're looking absolutely stunning.'

He took her to the Lobster Pot at L'Etacq.

'It's a seventeenth century farmhouse,' he told her, watching her delighted expression.

The granite building had retained its old world charm and from its windows were superb views of St. Ouen's bay.

'It's so unexpected,' she breathed, 'and what a wonderful view.'

Martin was pleased with himself. 'There you see, I knew just what you would like. It's got an international reputation.'

As she tackled a succulent lobster dish which was a speciality of the restaurant, Martin recounted yet more amusing anecdotes of his life as a banker and then went on to outline his ambitions and aspirations for the future. After a time he said, 'I'm sorry, Bethany, I must be boring you. My family tell me I like the sound of my own voice . . . so what about you? What have you got in mind for the next twenty years or so?'

She laughed and reaching across the table he placed his hand over hers and said, 'You've got such a lovely smile. I'm so glad you've come to Jersey. I couldn't wait to see you again.'

She ignored this, inwardly sighing as she

realised that any idea she might have had of a nice platonic relationship was about to be dispelled. She wondered, in fact, if there was any such thing. She just hoped that Martin wouldn't want to get too heavily involved and spoil things. She knew she liked him, but that was as far as it went so far as she was concerned. If she hadn't met Justin, then perhaps things might have been different.

'Why so solemn?' Martin asked. 'Surely thinking about your future can't be that sobering?'

She jerked herself back to the present and answering his question said,

'The fact is, Martin, I haven't a clue what I'm going to be doing beyond this year. The future of the bookshop has been a little uncertain recently.'

Martin poured some more of the excellent wine. 'Well, you're young enough to make the break if you need to. After all, in a few years time your sister will be old enough to fend for herself. I'm sure you could find yourself another librarian's post.'

'That's just it — I'm not at all sure that's what I want to do now . . . I feel I need to explore other options.' She told him about her painting and how she would quite like to do something that was art orientated.

It was quite late by the time they

195

had finished their meal which had been accompanied by music and dancing.

It was quite a while since Bethany had last been dancing and she thoroughly enjoyed herself, finding Martin a good partner but, in spite of their close proximity, she was not attracted to him in the way that she had been with Toby and could not even begin to compare him with Justin. She wondered what it would be like to dance with Justin . . .

'I beg your pardon — what did you say, Martin?'

'A penny for them — you seemed a million miles away just then. I actually asked you if you were thinking of going to the Battle of Flowers tomorrow?'

'Yes, we're joining forces with the Vautiers.'

'I see — I had rather hoped you'd come with me. I've managed to wangle a few more hours off.' He sounded disappointed.

'Well can't we all go together?' she suggested.

When they arrived back at Lilyville he walked with her to the front of the house and, catching her rather clumsily in his arms, kissed her on the mouth. It was not a heart-stopping kiss so far as she was concerned and the earth did not move for her, but it was tender and very satisfying to know that he cared for her and she responded in a similar manner, finding it a pleasant experience and a nice ending to what had been a most enjoyable evening.

Bethany stood on the steps waving to Martin as he drove away and, as she made to go into the house, Justin suddenly appeared from the shadows making her jump.

'Did you have a good evening?' he asked her casually.

'Yes, thanks — very,' she told him, wondering whether he had seen her locked in Martin's arms. Some of the shine left her, as she thought that if he had seen her then he obviously didn't care. It was as she had suspected. He was obviously arrogant enough to imagine that every girl he encountered desired him and had just viewed her as a plaything. Well, he was mistaken if he thought she was going to allow him to treat her like that. The problem was that she cared about his opinion of her and didn't want him to get the wrong impression. Why oh why was life so complicated?

On Thursday, as Bethany stood watching the Battle of Flowers Parade, she knew it was a spectacle that would stay with her for many months to come. She stood spellbound as countless floats, each covered with myriads of flowers, processed past. Each represented a different theme and the float had to be completely covered with flowers of a suitable colour and shape.

Martin took her arm and elbowed them forward to a more suitable vantage point. 'It's beautiful,' she breathed.

'Told you so! It's not like any other flower carnival in the world — look at that one made from wild flowers for instance! Not only do the entrants have to decorate their floats, but they also have to design them themselves — look at that entry from the General Hospital! This has been an annual event with only a break for war-time since 1902.'

'So there isn't actually a battle any more?' she asked.

'No, there used to be a flower fight, but nowadays we prefer to think of the carnival as a celebration — a reminder of the liberation of the Channel Islands from German occupation — but just you wait — there's more to come.'

Bethany realised how wonderful it would be to take part in something like that. There was such a community spirit and she tried to imagine how her grandmother must have felt, all those years ago, when she was evacuated to England from her beloved Jersey. Perhaps that had been the real problem — maybe Grandpa Tyler had not attempted to see things from his young wife's point of view — or appreciated how homesick she must have been.

Suddenly, as Bethany stood looking at the incredible array of brilliantly coloured floats decorated with a variety of flowers such as marigolds, carnations, hydrangeas — even thistles, she wondered if working with flowers was something she could do in the future. After all, she was already painting them so perhaps she could think of another idea.

'You're back in your dream world again,' Martin teased her.

'Actually, I've been thinking about my grandmother and how she must have felt about leaving her island and never knowing whether she would ever see it and her family again.'

'Yes, it's a sobering thought and there must have been countless others like your grandmother but — come on, this is a day for celebration. There will be parties later on . . . Oh, do look at that float representing the Jersey farmers. See, they've even incorporated vegetables in it. You know it takes the whole night to cover the float with their chosen design — imagine that.'

Bethany waved at a little girl dressed as a dairy maid. The intricate designs of the entries filled her with admiration.

At the end of the afternoon Bethany realised that they had become separated from the rest of their party, and she ended up going back with Martin to have tea with his parents in their pleasant house in St. Ouen.

Dr. and Mrs. Mauger were a delightful couple who couldn't have made her more welcome, telling her about various places of interest on the island and producing photographs of previous flower carnivals in which they themselves had participated. Presently Dr. Mauger was called out to one of his patients and, shortly afterwards, Martin drove her back to Lilyville. Sophie, spotting the car, invited him to stay for dinner, despite his protests that he was too casually dressed.

'We're eating early because Amber and James are going to a party at eight o'clock,' Sophie informed them. 'Justin's gone out already.'

When Bethany went upstairs to freshen up Amber joined her.

'So where were you after the Parade, Beth?' She looked quite put out. 'We hung about for ages, but we just couldn't see you anywhere.'

'I've told you — we lost you in the crowd.'

'Gave us the slip, more likely!' her sister retorted. 'Justin's gone to a party on the other side of the island. Some friends of his who were at Aunt Sophie's dinner party that evening, rang up just as we got back from the Parade. You were invited too, but none of us had a clue where you were, so he had to go without you . . . Honestly, Beth, I just can't understand what you see in Martin Mauger.'

Bethany looked at her sister in astonishment. 'I happen to find him very good company,' she said rather defensively. 'Anyway, whatever have you got against him?'

Amber tossed back her curls. 'Oh, nothing — it's just that he's so boring.'

'I don't think so. As a matter of fact, he's very knowledgeable about the island . . . Anyway, it's none of your business who I go out with . . . Now, tell me about this party you're going to with James.'

'Oh it's okay — some friends of the Vautiers, who happen to have teenagers about our age, are holding it. They've got a huge place, apparently, and so the olds are going to be in one room and we can use another . . . Now, don't look like that, Beth — no happy pills, no alcholic drink, I promise . . . Honestly you don't trust me at all, do you!'

'It doesn't have to be you,' Bethany pointed out wearily.

Tonight Amber seemed very grown up in a blue denim dress with her shining blonde hair arranged in a modern style. She stared defiantly at her sister.

'You just can't bear the idea of me having any fun, can you? What would you like me to do — stay at home and embroider a sampler? Daddy trusts me more than you do and, anyway, he's picking me up at eleven thirty, but I guess you'll be in bed by then drinking your cocoa!' And she went into her bedroom closing the door firmly behind her.

A dull ache filled Bethany as her thoughts turned to Justin. Had he really wanted her to accompany him to the party? Perhaps he hadn't seen Martin kissing her, after all. Maybe he did care for her just a little and now she had let the opportunity slide away.

'You're an idiot, Bethany Tyler,' she told herself aloud as she tidied her hair, 'and your little sister has better insight into situations than you do.' And then she thought of Martin waiting patiently for her to rejoin him downstairs. Poor Martin — was she just using him in an attempt to get back at Justin? She hoped he would regard their relationship as she was doing — as a holiday romance with no strings attached. Whatever happened she didn't want him to get the impression that she was leading him on.

Presently she went downstairs and made herself a charming companion to Martin throughout dinner. She caught Sophie looking at her once or twice, obviously wondering just how involved she was becoming with him.

For her part, however, Bethany was more concerned about Amber's infatuation with James. The boy had impeccable manners and it was obvious that her father was impressed by him. Tonight Amber looked positively blooming. Supposing she fell for James in a big way? After all, she was nearly sixteen and since she had been on Jersey suddenly seemed to have matured. It was a worrying thought.

Soon after the meal had ended the Vautiers turned up to collect James and Amber, and Martin, looking at his watch said, 'I'd better be making tracks too. I've just remembered that some friends of my father's are coming over this evening and I did promise to put in an appearance. Thanks for a lovely meal, Mrs. Le Claire!'

Martin did not kiss Bethany that evening, apart from a swift peck on the cheek, probably conscious that Sophie might be watching and she felt confused and unsettled by the events of the past few days. She still wasn't quite sure where Fenella Moignard fitted into Justin's life, but now he would be convinced that Bethany was involved with Martin and, perhaps it was just as well, because she couldn't bear to get hurt again. If only life weren't so complicated. It was a long time before she got to sleep that night.

The following morning Bethany collected her painting things and was just going into the garden when Justin came out of the study.

'Bethany, I've been thinking, I've promised to take you back to see Lily's cousin again, and she did say Friday would be a good time, so how about this morning?'

Bethany was surprised. 'I thought you had appointments all day.'

'I have, but they're a bit spread out and I've been wondering what we should do about Lily's cousin . . . I could drop you off and then come and pick you up in around an hour or so . . . also, if you've got some more paintings ready we could take them into the shop later on at Gorey.'

'Yes, all right then.' She tried not to sound too enthusiastic, even though her heart was pounding at the thought of spending some time with him. Presently they set off in the direction of St. Mary again.

Marjorie Touzel was delighted to see Bethany and, fortunately, the daughter-in-law had already gone shopping.

'That's good — now we can have a nice cup of tea,' the old lady said. 'She doesn't like me to keep putting the kettle on — always complaining about the cost of things she is . . . I'm sure she counts the teabags!'

Bethany laughed and went off to make the tea. Marjorie tucked into the cake Mrs. Vibert had sent when she learnt where Bethany was going.

'Rita don't let me have much cake — always on some fancy diet, she is. My Edward wasn't brought up that way, but at least he gets a square meal in his works' canteen so I don't have to worry about him.'

'You don't seem very happy, Mrs. Touzel,' Bethany ventured cautiously.

The old lady wiped a crumb from her chin. 'I thought it would be a good idea having them here to live with me. It didn't seem to be working out with her mother, but now I wish I'd kept my independence.'

'And I suppose there's no prospect of them getting their own place?'

Marjorie shook her head. 'Not at the moment with property being at such a premium, and I admit I do like a bit of company. It's been nice having Edward around but Rita and I don't see eye to eye. Anyway we can have a nice chat now she's gone out. You tell me all about Applebourne and Lily. I'd love to go and see her again, but it's been difficult. I thought it made sense giving them my money to look after, but now I'm not so sure.'

Bethany didn't like the sound of what Marjorie Touzel was telling her and wished Justin had been there to sum up the situation. She wondered what the son was like — weak by all accounts, she concluded. The daughter-in-law was so domineering that she obviously ruled the roost. Just what could be done she wasn't sure. After all, there were no obvious signs of neglect. Marjorie Touzel was living in a clean, comfortable environment and looked healthy enough. Bethany couldn't help wondering if the old lady might possibly be exaggerating the situation.

'Course I knew your grandmother,' she said, as Bethany washed the cups.

'Yes, Lily told me you were working at Swallowfield when my grandmother came to Applebourne.'

'That's right. She was Katherine Tyler

then, of course, such a beautiful lady she was — so, graceful and so kind. When she returned to Jersey she found me a position at Lilyville, and a couple of years later, I married the head gardener.'

Bethany was intrigued. 'And you obviously know Aunt Sophie too.'

'Oh yes, and that no good scallywag she married. What she ever saw in him I'll never know, but I suppose you can't choose who you fall in love with . . . '

That was true, Bethany acknowledged and checked that the kitchen was neat and tidy before returning to the sitting-room.

'And what about you, Miss Tyler? You're taken with that Mr. Rochel, aren't you? Stands out a mile and you make a lovely couple.'

Bethany protested, but the old lady just laughed. 'Whatever will be, will be — mind you, if he takes after his grandfather he won't go far wrong. Cedric Rochel was the nicest man you could ever wish to meet.'

The time flew past and, before long, Justin returned to collect Bethany. There was still no sign of the daughter-in-law.

'She'll have met up with one of her friends, no doubt. Well it's been lovely chatting — will you tell Lily her jumper fits a treat and I'll be getting in touch.'

The old lady stood waving as they drove off.

'So what did you think this time?' Justin asked.

Bethany recounted what Marjorie Touzel had said about her money.

He frowned. 'If I hadn't been dashing off to another appointment I'd have asked her a few questions myself. Anyway, we'll have to tread carefully . . . If only we could have a quiet word with the son then perhaps we could find out what the situation really is. Of course, it could just be the age old story of daughter-in-law and mother-in-law not hitting it off, but it's disturbing all the same.'

Their next port of call was to Gorey, an attractive village near to the sea with a row of white houses and a small harbour. Parking outside a little art and craft shop, Justin introduced Bethany to the owner and then excused himself saying he would return for her in about an hour.

Paul Le Brun was a large, good-looking man with a cultured voice and longish hair. He found Bethany a chair and then insisted on fetching her some coffee in a beautiful pottery mug.

'So you're the little lady who does these exquisite flower paintings. They've been selling like hot cakes, you know . . . Have you brought me any more?'

She handed him another four paintings. 'I'm sorry they haven't been framed.'

'That's no problem.' He paid her for the additional pictures he had managed to sell. 'So what brings you to Jersey? I gather you're staying with Justin Rochel.'

She explained briefly and he said. 'Nice guy, Justin . . . Seen anything of the delectable Fenella?'

She was startled. 'She was at Lilyville last week-end.'

He raised his eyebrows. 'Was she indeed. Now that she is — er free again, I suppose she and J.C. might just get back together again.'

He broke off as a customer came into the shop. It had been like having salt rubbed into a wound, Bethany thought. Just in case she had been likely to forget about Fenella Moignard — as if she could!

She wandered round the shop looking at the various trinkets and souvenirs of Jersey — all with quite high price tags. This merchandise was of a good quality and not the usual tourist trash. She felt pleased that Paul Le Brun thought her paintings were good enough to be included.

After a reasonable interval had elapsed, in

which Paul served two more customers and plied her with a number of anecdotes, she wished him goodbye and went out into the sunshine.

She wandered around Gorey ending up at the harbour where she stood looking at Mont Orgueil Castle standing like a sentinel over the eastern coastline. She knew that translated from the French it meant Mount Pride and wished there was time to look over it. Perhaps she could persuade Amber to come with her on another occasion. What a strange holiday this was turning out to be — not like anything she could ever have envisaged. She retraced her steps and returned to the shop to find Justin waiting for her.

'I've just about got time for lunch before my afternoon schedule,' he told her. He took her to 'The Secret Garden' near Gorey Common.

'Paul tells me your paintings are continuing to do well,' he said as they sat enjoying ploughman's lunches.

'Thank you, Justin. It was a brainwave of yours.' She handed him some notes. 'A bit more towards the wind-surfing lessons. Amber is having such a wonderful time and I'm so grateful to you.'

He rewarded her with one of his boyish

smiles. 'Don't be . . . She's a delightful girl and she's had a difficult time recently. I know you're worried in case her relationship with James gets too intense, but I don't think you need to be concerned because they're both very sensible youngsters . . . So tell me, what did you think of the Battle of Flowers yesterday?'

'It was quite wonderful . . . I'll always remember it.' Looking at him she added awkwardly, 'Justin, Amber's told me about the party invitation from your friends. I'm so sorry I didn't get back in time . . . '

His dark eyes were expressionless. 'It's no big deal — truly.'

She wanted to say, 'But I wouldn't have gone back with Martin had I realised,' but was determined not to show him how disappointed she had been. Let him think what he liked, she decided.

They finished the meal with coffee and then Justin said, 'I'm afraid I'm tied up from now on until around fourish . . . Did anyone think to tell you that we're all going for a picnic late afternoon? The Vautiers are joining us. We arranged it yesterday.'

She shook her head. 'No, but it sounds fun.'

Justin drove her into St. Helier and suggested she got a taxi back to Lilyville, but she opted for the bus. She had quite a walk from the bus stop, but as it was such a glorious afternoon she thoroughly enjoyed it.

When she arrived at the house she collected her grandmother's diaries and took them out onto the terrace. They spanned a period of about three years in all beginning in the year Katherine Tyler had returned to Jersey. Some entries were just daily records of what the family had had for dinner etc. but as Bethany read on, a much clearer picture emerged of what had happened between her grandparents.

By the time she had finished the first one she realised that Katherine had felt repressed and misunderstood. She had obviously been an extremely sociable lady who had loved entertaining and going to parties, but Grandpa Tyler had wanted none of this. He had found his wife extravagant, but she had found him penny pinching. There was also another issue — even in those days Katherine had felt that her husband favoured Peter and had little time for Sophie.

Katherine had been homesick and had longed to spend some time with her family in Jersey, but Grandpa Tyler had wanted her to put her former life behind her. When she had tried discussing things he had refused to listen, but then had come the final showdown when he had told her, 'Go then and take that snivelling child with you!' And so Katherine had gone to Lilyville with Sophie and had never returned.

Of course words were often spoken in anger, but, as Bethany read on things gradually began to fall into place in her mind . . . She looked up as Amber rushed onto the terrace.

'Where's Daddy?'

'I think he and Aunt Sophie are in the sitting-room. Why? What's the urgency?'

'The Vautiers are going sailing for the week-end and they've asked me to join them.' She caught Bethany's rather disapproving look. 'It's all right, I'll be back before Aunt Sophie goes into hospital on Tuesday. I haven't forgotten — I'm sure Daddy will say, 'Yes' . . . What are all those dusty old books?'

Without giving Bethany a chance to reply she scooped one up. 'Grandma's diaries, what fun!' She read out an extract. 'Today Cedric took me to St. Clement's Bay for a picnic. We had an enchanting time and he kissed me. I think I'm falling in love with him!' Whow that's romantic stuff! I still don't understand why she and Grandpa didn't get divorced.'

Bethany retrieved the diary. 'Divorce

wasn't something you took so lightly as people do nowadays and, anyway, remember that for the first eighteen months after she returned to Jersey, she truly believed Grandpa Tyler would relent and come after her. This is a later diary, written after she had given up hope of him ever wanting her back.'

Amber frowned. 'That makes Grandpa sound mean and I've never thought of him in that way.'

'Then don't — remember him as you knew him. What happened in the past between your grandparents need not colour the memories you have of either of them — just remember the good times we spent together.'

'Thanks, Beth, you always could put things in perspective for me . . . See you presently,' and Amber practically skipped back into the house.

Bethany was filled with a strange mixture of emotions. There was certainly no need to disillusion her young sister about their grandparents, but if she had read things correctly then there were even more revelations to come. She wondered if Justin and Aunt Sophie had read all the diaries or if they had just passed them over to her. Delving into the past could be a bittersweet experience, as she was beginning to learn, and perhaps it would be best to leave well alone.

9

On the way to Ouaisné Bay for the picnic
Sophie suddenly said, 'I've encountered
a problem regarding next week — I'd
completely forgotten Mary Vibert is having
her holiday then. Normally it wouldn't matter
as I'd be perfectly happy to do all the cooking,
but it could be difficult to get someone in at
such short notice . . . I hate leaving you all
to fend for yourselves but . . . '

'Don't worry,' Bethany told her. 'I'm not
a very good cook, but I can manage — I'll
try not to poison anyone!'

Justin laughed. 'You've changed your tune.
When we first met, if looks could have killed,
I'd have been dead several times over.'

'You're exaggerating, Justin! It wasn't like
that at all,' she protested.

'I can't let you do the cooking, Bethany,
you're a guest.'

'We'll all lend a hand, Sophie,' Justin
assured her. 'As you know my speciality
is breakfast — oh and spaghetti bolognaise
— and I know Bethany is good with
casseroles and apple pies because I've
sampled them.'

'And I can do my tuna bake,' volunteered Amber.

'We'll manage, Sophie,' Peter said. 'And if we get tired of eating in then we'll eat out. There are plenty of good restaurants, as you keep telling me.'

Sophie seemed reassured and Bethany settled back to look at the scenery. From time to time she stole a surreptitious glance as Justin, noting the way his hair curved into the nape of his neck, and his strong tanned hands on the wheel.

Before long they arrived at Ouiasnés Bay which boasted a delightful sandy beach that was a suntrap in the afternoon. A picnic, Aunt Sophie fashion, meant doing things in style and took quite a lot of setting up. When Justin opened the boot he revealed chairs and a picnic table complete with a sparkling white tablecloth and napkins, a large hamper and several cool boxes containing everything that they could possibly need. They had just about got things organised to Sophie's satisfaction when the Vautiers turned up.

The picnic was everything anyone could have wished for — fresh salmon, potatoes with soured cream, and salad, washed down by ice-cold fruit wine. All this was followed by strawberries, a selection of sumptuous gateaux and flasks of tea. Afterwards, the youngsters volunteered to pack away, whilst the older members of the party soon became engaged in their favourite occupation of setting the world to rights. Turning to Bethany, Justin said sotto voce:

'Do you fancy a little leg stretch?' And, smilingly, she got to her feet and they set off along the beach. He pointed out the direction of the prehistoric cave-dwelling.

'It's the site of La Cotte de St. Brelade, a Stone Age lair,' he explained. 'It was discovered in 1881 and countless archaeologists have been there since. They've found bones of extinct animals such as the woolly rhinoceros and the mammoth to say nothing of the remains of Mousterian men.'

'Can you go into the cave?' she asked, fascinated.

He shook his head. 'Nope, it's closed to the public, but years back, when Prince Charles was at Cambridge, he came here and joined in the dig.'

'It must be wonderful to find something so old.'

'Yes, it makes one humble to think that we're only here on this earth for such a relatively short time and to know that all those years ago, others probably walked on this very same beach.'

'I wonder what early man would think if

he came back now and saw the car park and the cafés . . . Haven't we ruined things with commercialization?'

'You have to have progress, Beth.' It was the first time he had used the diminutive and, almost without thinking, she slipped her arm through his.

'Yes, and change . . . I suppose things can't stay the same for ever.'

'No — that's why I hope you'll come to accept what has happened regarding Swallowfield and Lilyville.'

She stared at him. 'Nice one — I wondered when we'd get round to that subject again.'

'Well, we can't go on avoiding the issue — anyway, I thought you were fairly reconciled to what's happening.'

'I suppose I'm going to have to be, as there's no alternative.'

She withdrew her arm abruptly. 'There are, however, quite a few things that I don't understand.'

'Give me a for instance.' His rich brown eyes searched her face.

'Aunt Sophie still seems to be incredibly extravagant . . . '

'Yes, I've told you before that both she and your grandmother enjoyed a high standard of living.'

'That's one way of putting it, I suppose,

but, even now, she doesn't seem to be making any attempt to economise.'

'In order to make that assumption you would have needed to have known her lifestyle before my grandfather died.'

'Are you telling me that it was more lavish than this?' she demanded.

He drew a semi-circle in the sand with the toe of his shoe. C for Cedric, she wondered.

'Yes, considerably so. She would have dined out frequently in expensive restaurants and entertained on the scale you have seen very regularly. She spent a small fortune on beauty products and clothes, ran up amazing bills with Fenella, and flew over to the other islands and St. Malo whenever she felt like it, to see various friends . . . '

'Beside hers, our lifestyle is positively frugal,' Bethany said with a tinge of bitterness, 'and yet we are the ones that have been faced with selling Swallowfield and have had to make the sacrifices. Dad's sold nearly all his collection of first editions recently to a rich acquaintance of your St. Malo friends . . . did you know that?'

Justin inclined his head. 'No, I'm sorry, I didn't but hasn't it occurred to you that, maybe there are other reasons for your father's current financial problems? Perhaps if you talked to him . . . '

Bethany frowned, wondering what he was driving at. 'I don't need to — he's always been open with me. I'm fully aware that he lost out on some of his investments a few years back. We had to pull our horns in quite considerably then and so, this time round, there's been very little else that we could cut back on . . . Anyway, what I still don't understand is why Cedric cut Aunt Sophie off without a penny . . . '

'Then I'll tell you!' His dark eyes were suddenly blazing. 'My grandfather gave Sophie a very generous allowance every year after Katherine died, and she waded through it so that there was never anything left in her bank balance after a few months and she frequently became overdrawn. Now, perhaps, you'll understand why he simply arranged that I should just take care of her daily needs and give her precious little to live on. In all fairness, Sophie is a very generous, warm-hearted person and she has never used the money entirely for herself. Playing the Lady Bountiful is very commendable, but she simply doesn't know when to stop . . . '

Bethany swallowed hard. 'I don't believe you!'

Justin threw up his hands in a gesture of impatience. 'Then why don't you ask her? If you want the answers and then choose not to believe them, because they are not what you wish to hear, then there's not a lot I can do about it. I am very fond of Sophie, as I was of Katherine, and I get on well with your father too — but when it comes down to money matters, none of them has been able to discipline themselves in order to prevent getting into financial difficulties . . . '

'You can't include my father in that — I won't let you!' she practically shouted at him.

'Suit yourself, but one day, Bethany Tyler, you will realise that I am right. You can't just use your intuition. When you've got all your facts straight come back to me and we'll discuss matters further. Until then, perhaps you should leave well alone and accept that the decisions that have been made, regarding Swallowfield and Lilyville, were in the very best interests of all concerned.'

'Made in your very best interests, you mean,' she said furiously and hurried back along the beach, the tears stinging her eyes.

He was perfectly hateful, she told herself and had thoroughly deserved that last remark. Whatever was he insinuating? Her father had never run up debts or squandered money. They had scrimped and scraped over the years in order to pay the bills and maintain

Swallowfield, and now, Justin Rochel — a perfect stranger, who did not have any money worries, had come into their lives and somehow taken control and, in doing so, had managed to devalue everything that she held dear. The future, which a few days ago had seemed rosy, suddenly appeared bleak.

The next morning Bethany came downstairs to find Amber breakfasting on waffles and honey — something that James and Charlotte had introduced her to, apparently.

'I told you Daddy would be cool about my going sailing, didn't I?'

'And what about Aunt Sophie? Are you intending to say goodbye to her before you disappear for the week-end?'

Amber scowled at her sister. 'Oh, don't give me a hard time, Beth!'

Their father came into the room at that juncture.

'Surely you two aren't quarrelling?'

Bethany poured him some tea. 'Just a slight difference of opinion.'

'Beth doesn't think I should go off for the week-end,' Amber threw out

Peter helped himself to a bowl of cereal and then, looking at Bethany said, 'I've already told Amber that I don't mind her going if Sophie doesn't. She might as well make the most of the good weather . . . Just

222

take care, darling, that's all we ask.'

Bethany decided it would be foolish to say anything further, but she had an uncomfortable feeling about the way things were developing between her sister and James Vautier.

When Justin returned from driving Amber over to the Vautiers he came to find Bethany in the summer house.

'Olivia's been up half the night with Charlotte who has a bad gastric attack. I offered to bring James and Amber back here, but Rupert said he'll take the pair of them sailing — even if it's only for a few hours.'

'Oh, poor Charlotte — what a shame.'

'Yes, they've called the doctor just as a precaution. Rupert said he'd leave us a message on the answer phone if he decided to bring Amber back this evening.' He paused and then said, 'We're going out to lunch at Rozel — if you'd care to join us. It's one of Sophie's favourite spots.'

'I'd like that,' she replied, seeing it as an olive branch after their disagreement at Ouaisné Bay.

Rozel turned out to be a charming fishing hamlet. They had an early lunch at Le Couperon with its restaurant in an indoor vinery. As she sat enjoying the delicious seafood, Bethany realised that she was beginning to relax again. She half regretted her outburst of the previous day, but then decided that it was surely better to air ones differences and Justin didn't seem to hold it against her. He caught her gaze now and gave her a devastating smile that made her heart pound uncontrollably. Raising his glass he said, 'To Sophie — may her health soon improve.'

'To Sophie,' they echoed.

After the meal, Justin drove them to The Orchid Trust in Victoria Village, Trinity.

'It's one of the best collections in Europe,' Sophie said, 'I never tire of coming here and knowing your love of flowers, Bethany, I thought you'd enjoy it too. It was formerly the private collection of the late Eric Young and there's now a foundation to carry on with his work.'

The beauty of the delicate wax-like blooms took Bethany's breath away. The collection, which had opened to the public in 1986, filled several tropical houses together with a landscaped display area.

Her father smiled indulgently as she stood enraptured. 'I've never seen so many different specimens . . . This is a wonderful surprise — thank you, Justin.'

'Oh, I can't take the credit. It was Sophie's

idea, but I'm so glad you've enjoyed it
. . . plenty of inspiration for some more
paintings, eh? I bet if you had a word with
someone in charge you'd be allowed to bring
your sketch book here sometime.'

She nodded, stars in her eyes. Suddenly
all was right with her world again.

They hadn't been back at Lilyville for long,
however, when the phone rang. Bethany
was in the hall when Justin returned from
answering it, looking extremely grim.

'That was Rupert Vautier on the phone
. . . apparently he stayed behind, after all,
because Charlotte was so poorly that she
was admitted to hospital late morning. He
thought Amber and James were coming
straight back here, but obviously they haven't
shown up or they would have left us a
message — and now, he's realised 'The
Seagull' has gone missing.'

Bethany's stomach turned over. 'Surely
you're not telling me . . .'

He nodded. 'I'm finding it hard to believe
myself, but it rather looks as though they've
gone off on the yacht on their own!'

She swallowed. 'I know Amber can be
strong-willed, but I really wouldn't have
thought she'd be capable of something quite
so foolhardy . . . Whatever are we going to
do, Justin?'

'A, keep calm, B, don't let's trouble Sophie — although I appreciate your father will need to know, of course. I know it's difficult, but we must be patient and let Rupert deal with the situation as he thinks best. At present, he's still hoping that they'll return of their own accord when they've come to their senses.'

'Can James handle the yacht?' she asked fearfully.

'Hopefully, yes.' Bethany bit her lip and he caught her to him.

'It'll be all right, Beth. We must hope they'll have the good sense to radio in for help if they need it and that they'll behave responsibly.'

Peter Tyler looked grave when he heard the news. 'I'm sorry, Beth, I really am . . . I should have listened to you. I know Amber is practically sixteen, but I just can't stop thinking of her as my little girl, still.'

'I feel we ought to be doing something — rather than just sitting here twiddling our thumbs,' Bethany said, a sick feeling in the pit of her stomach.

'I really think we should leave it to Rupert,' Justin repeated. 'He'll know what to do and will contact the right authorities without hesitation, when and if necessary . . . Apparently, they went down to the boat to collect something, saying that they'd be coming over here afterwards for a swim. I can only assume that they came out with this story thinking no-one would check on them for a few hours. I'm sure they'll be back when the novelty wears off and, in the meantime, I'm afraid there's precious little we can do but wait.'

Bethany knew he was talking sense, but felt helpless all the same and it was difficult keeping up a pretence of normality in front of Sophie. It was like a nightmare and, eventually, she excused herself, saying that she had a headache and went to her room.

Sleep evaded Bethany that night. She offered up a prayer and immediately felt a little calmer. Around dawn she went downstairs to make herself a cup of tea and found Justin already in the kitchen.

'Hallo, someone else who couldn't sleep either.' He poured her a mug of tea. 'Young scallywags — if only they knew the worry they're causing us!' He put an arm about her waist. 'I'm sure they won't come to any harm, Beth. Rupert Vautier will have a strong talk with James when he returns and, in the meantime, we must just hope that he behaves in a responsible fashion towards your sister.'

'Like you are towards me?' she asked.

'You're different. You're over sixteen.' The kiss that he gave her was very comforting and filled her with warmth. 'Even your hair smells of flowers,' he said, as he caught long silky tendrils between his fingers. He released her abruptly, however, as his mobile phone rang.

It was Rupert Vautier saying that there was no news and that they were becoming increasingly concerned, as they felt that James would have had the good sense to have returned by now.

'Rupert's decided it's time to report 'The Seagull' officially missing,' Justin informed her. 'He feels it would be irresponsible to leave it any longer . . . I'm going off to meet up with him now.'

'Then I'm coming with you . . . just give me a few minutes to dress.'

Justin had arranged to meet Rupert Vautier at the marina where 'The Seagull' had been moored. He was looking thunderous.

'I simply cannot credit that James could be such a crass idiot! He knew how worried we already were about Charlotte — without this.'

'How is she now?' Bethany asked, realising that poor Charlotte had been pushed to the back of her mind during this new crisis.

'Much better, but the hospital have kept

228

her in overnight for observation. It seems that it's almost certainly a grumbling appendix.'

Bethany had just turned away from the spot where the yacht should have been moored when she kicked something with the toe of her shoe. Frowning, she picked the object up and turned it over in her hand.

'It's Amber's Alice band . . . She was wearing it yesterday morning.'

'She must have dropped it,' Justin said, somewhat dismissively.

'No, I'm sure she wouldn't have been that careless. It's of sentimental value — our mother bought it for her . . . unless, of course, she dropped it deliberately . . . '

He was staring at her, trying to understand her reasoning. 'What exactly are you saying, Beth?'

'All along we've believed Amber and James have gone off together on the boat — but, just supposing, we've got it all wrong and that someone else made them take it out against their will . . . I know it's a long shot, but it's almost as if the Alice band is Amber's way of — of letting us know what's happening.'

'Of course,' Rupert Vautier said. 'Why on earth didn't we think of that possibility before? Maybe someone was in need of an escape route off the island or, more likely, some lads wanted a joy ride. Anyway, your theory has put a totally different complexion on things . . . I'm going back to the car to do some more phoning!'

Bethany put the hair band safely in her shoulder bag. 'If anything's happened to them it'll be our fault for not trusting them. We ought to have reported the yacht missing hours ago . . . ' Her voice broke.

Justin slipped an arm about her shoulder. 'No-one's to blame, Beth. We don't know for sure what's happened and Rupert will make sure that all the right authorities are contacted . . . '

He trailed off and she saw the expression on his face change.

'What is it, Justin?'

'It's just occured to me that perhaps they're not on 'The Seagull' at all. What if they've been locked up somewhere so that they can't raise the alarm?'

It was practically three hours later when the police found Amber safe and well in a disused warehouse. When the news came through, Sophie was in the kitchen organising lunch with the help of Bethany and Nicki. She was astounded.

'You mean to say all this has been going on and you haven't seen fit to tell me? Whyever not, may I ask? Thank God the child is safe and well.'

Peter went down to the police station to be with Amber and when eventually she returned shaken, dirty, but otherwise none the worse for her adventure, she was made such a fuss of that she couldn't believe it.

'Perhaps I should get locked up more often,' she quipped.

It was as Justin had eventually figured out; Amber had been locked up to prevent her from raising the alarm. The men who had taken 'The Seagull' had been unable to man her however, and so James was still with them. Amber had been told that if she tried to attract attention too soon James would be harmed. Judging from a conversation she had overheard, her captor was probably still on the island.

It was early evening when James rang his grandfather to say that he had been picked up by some fishermen off the coast of France. He had been put overboard in the yacht's inflatable dinghy.

Much later as they sat over a very belated evening meal, Amber said, 'Perhaps you'll believe that I can be trusted from now on. Honestly, if James and I had intended to go off for a week-end together, do you think we'd have been so mad as to have taken

'The Seagull'? Give us some credit.'

'So let's get this straight,' Sophie recapped. 'Charlotte is in hospital with suspected appendicitis, James is in France having had a brush with some criminals and you've been locked up in a warehouse — and, whilst all this has been going on, I've been blissfully unaware of any of it.'

Peter patted her on the shoulder. 'Never mind — all's well that ends well.'

Bethany hoped they would never have to relive another week-end like this one. Suddenly the realisation of what might have happened hit her and, with a mumbled apology, she got up from the table and went upstairs to her room.

The tears flowed then and she was powerless to stop them. After a few minutes, there was a gentle tap on the door and Justin came in.

'I know I'm probably intruding, but I wanted to see if you were all right . . . Hey what's all this — it's not as bad as all that, you know.'

And, before she realised it, she was in the shelter of his arms and he was stroking her hair and murmuring tender endearments. He kissed away the tears and then his lips met hers and suddenly everything was all right again.

His kisses set her on fire. His hands moved sensuously over her breasts making her want to cry out. As he held her close against him, she experienced a kaleidoscope of exquisite sensations and knew that she desired him as she had never desired any other man.

It was he who moved away. 'You're in an emotional state and it would be wrong for me to take advantage,' he said gruffly. 'Everything will be just fine, you'll see . . . ' And, abruptly, he went from the room, leaving her feeling more confused than ever.

There was no sign of Justin at breakfast the next morning.

'He's had to see some clients on Guernsey, so he's made an early start,' Peter informed Bethany. 'If you remember he only arranged to take a few days off initially and so he's got a backlog of work to catch up on.'

Bethany felt relieved for it gave her a bit of space to pull herself together after the previous evening.

Amber seemed none the worse for her ordeal, but Dr. Mauger advised keeping her quiet for a couple of days which was easier said than done. She moped about the house like a caged animal and it was just as well that the weather was rather inclement. Bethany persuaded her to help in the kitchen and this took her mind off things for a time.

Rupert Vautier had gone to France to be with James who had had to undergo a certain amount of questioning by the French police.

On Tuesday morning Peter drove Sophie to the hospital. Although she put a brave face on it, Bethany suspected that inwardly she was very frightened. They stayed with her until she had settled in and were told that her operation was scheduled for the following afternoon.

Bethany found it a busy day, cooking for the family and sorting out various other domestic matters with Nicki, the daily help.

James had returned to Jersey, but had managed to develop a chill and so was also confined to barracks for a few days, which made Amber even more gloomy. She brightened up considerably, however, when she learnt that the French police had caught up with the criminals who had taken 'The Seagull', and that they had been found in possession of a quantity of stolen jewellery which they had been hoping to off-load on the continent. The third member of the trio turned out to be someone who the Jersey police had been keeping under surveillance for a long while, and he was apprehended in St. Clement.

That afternoon a reporter came round

234

from 'The Jersey Evening Post,' to interview Amber, bringing a photographer with him. She was thrilled.

Justin had gone off on business again early that morning, saying that he would return in time for dinner and would call in to see Sophie en route. But, in the event, he changed his plans.

Amber took the phone call and came into the kitchen to tell Bethany.

'Justin says he's sorry, but he'll be eating out, after all, this evening — something's come up.'

Perhaps it was just as well, Bethany reflected as she served a rather mediocre chicken casserole. They were just finishing the meal when the phone rang again. This time it was Fenella Moignard wanting to speak to Justin. She sounded surprised when Bethany answered.

'He's not there? Oh, never mind — I'll try to get him on his mobile. He's meeting me at the airport and needs to know the time of my flight . . . Look, I've got to go now — 'bye.'

So Fenella Moignard was the 'something' that had come up! Bethany might have known that it wouldn't be long before she put in an appearance again.

Bethany went into the kitchen and began

to stack the dishwasher, her mind filled with rather uncharitable thoughts about Fenella. She found herself wishing that they hadn't agreed to stay on at Lilyville, and realised that Fenella and Justin were probably wishing the same thing, for then they could have had the place to themselves.

Bethany heard Justin return from his rendezvous with Fenella at around midnight. She lay awake into the early hours of the morning trying to come to terms with the situation. She sighed as she remembered Justin's kisses, realising that he had managed to leave her feeling emotionally fragile yet again.

Sophie's operation went ahead as scheduled the following afternoon and, afterwards, Peter went to the hospital to sit with her for a while.

It had been an odd sort of day. After organising dinner, Bethany decided to finish one of her paintings before reading another diary and some of her grandmother's letters. At five o'clock, however, Fenella turned up in a taxi. Bethany tried not to register her surprise as the driver brought in the luggage. Fenella swept up the steps looking extremely chic in an emerald-green two piece.

'Bethany, darling, you can't imagine the appalling time I've had. The hotel I've been staying in is overflowing with tourists and I really can't bear to be there another minute, so Justin has insisted I come here. At the end of the day I don't suppose one more house-guest will make much difference, will it?'

Bethany pulled herself together sufficiently to explain that Mrs. Vibert was on holiday. Surely Justin couldn't have overlooked that small point?

'Oh, but I wouldn't want to put you to any trouble on my account,' Fenella said sweetly. 'Why don't I just choose one of the spare rooms, and the maid — whatever her name is — can make up the bed.'

Bethany was tempted to tell her to make up her own bed — for poor Nicki was already doing a great many extra jobs. With a great deal of restraint, Bethany said, 'I'll see what I can do . . . Would you like some tea?'

'Providing it's Earl Grey.'

Amber followed Bethany into the kitchen. 'What's she doing here?' she asked in a fierce whisper.

Bethany explained briefly and then gave her attention to the chicken curry which should just about stretch to an extra one if she cooked plenty of rice. She had just finished knocking up a reasonable-looking fruit salad when Justin poked his head round the door.

'I've just called in at the hospital, but Sophie was asleep so I only stayed for a few minutes . . . Your father says not to wait dinner . . . Thank you for looking after Fenella — apparently, her hotel was rather crowded and uncomfortable, so she'll be staying here for the time being. She's rather anxious to see Sophie tomorrow afternoon, so I've said I'll take her then and perhaps you won't mind going in the evening — if that's okay.'

It would have to be, Bethany thought crossly. She stirred the contents of the saucepan vigorously.

As they sat down to the meal in the dining room, Fenella wrinkled her nose and said, 'I'm afraid I don't eat curry, but don't worry I'll make do with vegetables and rice.'

Justin sprang to his feet. 'You most certainly will not — we've plenty of ham in the fridge and some cold pork.'

'I'll get it,' Bethany said, fuming inwardly.

'Oh, dear, am I being a nuisance? Sophie knows my little fads, you see. She and I both find curry a little indigestible.'

'That's the trouble with getting old,' Amber said, 'you have to watch your digestion.'

Fenella turned pink and Bethany hastily took a sip of water for fear of laughing.

'Amber thinks anyone over eighteen is

drawing her old age pension,' Justin said, a twinkle in his eyes.

During most of the main course, Fenella talked to Justin about people they both knew — deliberately excluding Bethany and Amber from the conversation. She did, however, show a brief interest in Amber's escapade with 'The Seagull'. Fortunately, Fenella ate fruit salad and the rest of the meal passed without further incident. They were drinking coffee in the sitting room when Peter Tyler returned. Bethany thought he looked tired and rather drawn. If he were surprised to see Fenella, he did not show it.

'Sophie's still very drowsy after the anaesthetic and, obviously, in quite a bit of pain,' he said in response to their questions. 'I haven't been able to speak to a doctor, as yet, to ask how the operation went and, obviously, the nurses won't give too much away . . . '

'Poor Sophie,' Fenella sympathised. 'Did my flowers arrive?'

'I did see some flowers, but I have to admit, I didn't discover who they were from.'

Bethany got to her feet and collected up the empty coffee cups. After a few minutes Amber joined her in the kitchen.

'I can't believe Justin's asked Fenella to

stay . . . She's obviously not going to lift a finger.'

Bethany managed to say composedly enough, 'Well, it is Justin's house, love, and he is entitled to ask whoever he likes to stay. After all we are his guests too — remember!'

It was going to be painful watching the two of them together, Bethany realised. She wondered what Fenella would say if she ever found out that Justin had kissed her, but perhaps that was the whole idea — perhaps Justin wanted to make Fenella jealous.

10

Dr. Mauger rang up later that evening wanting to speak to Justin. After a few minutes, Justin called Bethany to the 'phone, telling her that Martin would like a quick word.

'How are you, with all that's been going on?' Martin wanted to know.

'Fine,' she told him. They chatted for a few moments about the events of the past few days and then he asked:

'I suppose it's out of the question to see you at the moment? When are you visiting Mrs. Le Claire?'

'Tomorrow evening — apparently Justin and Fenella are going tomorrow afternoon.'

'Fenella! So she's around again, is she?'

'Yes. Actually, she's staying here for a few days.'

'You should be so lucky . . . How about lunch tomorrow, then?'

'I'd love to, Martin,' Bethany said on impulse.

'Wonderful — if you could get yourself into St. Helier.' He explained to her where to find the bank and gave her the 'phone number in case of emergencies.

When she returned to the sitting room, Justin said, 'It was good of Dr. Mauger to ring, wasn't it? He knew how worried we were.' In response to her enquiry he added, 'He's been in touch with the hospital and they've said the operation went well.'

Bethany felt a surge of relief. 'That's good news.'

'What did Martin want?' Amber asked in that direct way of hers.

'To ask me out to lunch tomorrow, as a matter of fact . . . Will you all be able to manage here?'

As she had thought, they were all planning to be out for lunch anyway.

Presently Peter Tyler went off to the study and Justin got to his feet too. 'If you'll excuse me there are some rather pressing 'phone calls to make. My answer-phone tape is rapidly filling up.'

'Well, in that case, I might as well catch up on a little of my own paper work,' Fenella said. 'Could you look over my accounts for me, darling?'

They went out of the room together and Amber turned to Bethany. 'Could you look at my anorak for me, darling?' she asked in a perfect mimicry of Fenella.

'Hush, she'll hear you — anyway, what's

wrong with your anorak?'

'It got caught on a nail in that wretched warehouse and you know what my needlework is like.'

As Bethany examined the tear, Amber said, 'Why do you let Fenella Whatsername, walk all over you?'

Bethany chose to ignore this remark and concentrated on the garment in front of her. 'I may need to get something to patch this. It would be your new one.'

Amber was persistent. 'So why are you going out with Martin, and letting Fenella take Justin right from under your very nose?'

'I've told you before, Martin and I are just friends — not that it's any of your business,' Bethany told her sister rather sharply.

Amber shook her head. 'You're impossible, Beth! I thought you really liked Justin!' She hesitated and then said, 'I thought perhaps we could go for a ride sometime. We never seem to do anything together these days.'

And with this surprising comment, she went out of the room. Could it be that Amber had turned to James and the Vautier family because her own family had been neglecting her in some way? Full of misgivings about the way things were turning out since they had been at Lilyville, Bethany picked up the anorak and went upstairs. As she passed the first landing, she heard laughter coming from the direction of the office. Far from doing any work they seemed to be sharing a joke together.

Once in the privacy of her own room, she sank onto the bed and stared into space. Justin could not have made it any clearer that their relationship had meant nothing to him. She ought to have known by now that practically any man, given the encouragement, would flirt. And, after all, how could she expect him to care for her when they came from such totally different backgrounds?

She had tried hard to deny the extent of her feelings for him — to tell herself that it was just because she was feeling so vulnerable — but she knew now that she had fallen in love with Justin Rochel. There was a pain in her throat as she wondered how he would react if he had any idea of the way she felt about him.

When Justin rang the hospital the following morning, he was told that Sophie was as comfortable as could be expected. After breakfast, Bethany took herself into St. Helier. There were a few things she needed from the shops before she met up with Martin for lunch.

To her surprise, as she was window-shopping in King Street she saw Lily's cousin walking rather wearily towards her. She called out and the old lady's face brightened.

'Well, if it isn't Miss Tyler. I was just thinking about you and here you are.'

'It's lovely to see you,' Bethany said. 'Have you got time for a cup of coffee?'

'I'd like that — as it happens, I've got a bit of time to kill before my son picks me up.'

Marjorie Touzel steered Bethany into a nearby café and over coffee and Jersey Wonders — a kind of doughnut shaped like a figure of eight and recommended by Mrs. Touzel — they had an interesting conversation.

'It's been difficult to know where to turn these past few months,' the old lady confided. 'I've been so worried about money matters and either my Edward hasn't been so honest with me as he ought to have been, or else he doesn't know what his wife's been getting up to. That Rita's been running up debts and using the money I've been giving her to pay the bills for other things . . . I only found out by accident when I opened a letter addressed to her by mistake the other day.'

Bethany sipped her coffee, realising that this could explain a great deal.

245

'So what are you going to do about it?'

The old lady shrugged. 'There's not a lot I can do, unless my Edward believes me. He won't hear a word said against her . . . Anyway, I'm going to tell him straight that unless he sorts things out, he'll have to find alternative accommodation . . . I'm going to ring Lily soon, but I don't want them to know. I have to be ever so careful about using the 'phone. Rita's always listening in and complaining about the expense.'

'I'm sorry you're having such a hard time, but, at least, it will be for the best if you contact Lily.'

'Don't you worry about me, Miss Tyler. There are worse things happening at sea . . . Oh, fancy me saying that after the trouble you had with your young sister and those criminals.'

News certainly got around. They spent a few moments discussing what had happened and then Bethany told her about Aunt Sophie being in hospital.

'Poor Mrs. Le Claire . . . She always was rather on the delicate side. Mr. Rochel was so protective towards her — treated her just like his own daughter. They were such a lovely family and so happy when the baby came along . . . '

'They had a child!' Bethany exclaimed.

Mrs. Touzel looked awkward. 'If I've spoken out of turn then I'm sorry. The past is the past and, I suppose, we oughtn't to go raking it up . . . As the years went by people looked upon your grandmother and Cedric Rochel as man and wife. Of course, in this day and age no-one would think twice about the situation . . . It would be nice to think you and young Mr. Rochel were going to be friends . . . ' She paused significantly, leaving Bethany in absolutely no doubt as to what she meant.

'Oh, we only met each other a couple of months back.'

'Sometimes you don't have to know a person for that long to realise there's something good going for you. My husband and I — we knew right away and, so too, did your grandmother and Cedric Rochel.'

Mrs. Touzel picked up her shopping bag. 'Now, I did enjoy this coffee and the chat. It's cheered me up no end, my dear. Thank you so much.'

Bethany insisted upon paying the bill and they parted company outside the shop. Marjorie Touzel had certainly given her something to think about. Things had been so busy at Lilyville just recently that she had not found time to read any more of the diaries, and she hadn't even looked at the letters. Now she was almost afraid of what she might discover — of what new revelations lay in store.

Martin was ten minutes late for their rendezvous and looked a little harrassed. 'Let's go eat. I'm starving!' he informed her. 'How about some genuine fish and chips?'

He took her to Albert J. Ramsbottom's well known fish and chip restaurant which was teeming with tourists. It was so unexpected and so different from the other places she had been taken to so far.

'I knew you'd like it,' he told her. 'Almost everyone I know does and I have to admit a passion for fish and chips — especially after the sort of morning I've just had!'

As they sat enjoying their meal and discussing the events of the past week, she felt herself relaxing. After they had finished he said,

'Now, I've just about got time to take you on a short sight-seeing trip before my meeting at three o'clock . . . I've no end of time owing to me and so I'm entitled to an occasional extended lunch break. Incidentally, Fenella came into the bank this morning, looking as if she'd just come from the beautician's.'

'She probably had — after all she is a beauty consultant and does know how to make the best of herself.'

'I wonder what she looks like without her make-up?'

'That's unkind, Martin,' she rebuked him gently . . . 'Where are we going?'

He drove her to St. Matthew's Church at Millbrook — somewhere Bethany had mentioned that she wanted to visit.

'You remembered!' she exclaimed, pleased.

He took her arm and they went into the rather ordinary looking church which he told her was built in 1840. However, it was the interior with its delicate glass work by Rene Lalique of Paris that made it so famous.

'Impressive isn't it? It seems that Lalique took the secret of manufacturing this special glass to the grave with him.'

'It's beautiful,' she agreed, admiring the fifteen feet high glass cross dominating the chancel.

'Very often that's lit up during worship . . . Take a look at the glass font. It's probably the only one in existence.'

The Glass Church, as it was popularly known, captured Bethany's artistic imagination. Besides the windows and the side screens, two altars and some angels in the Lady Chapel were all made of the unique glass.

Presently, Bethany went to stand in front of one of the altars and offered up a prayer for

Aunt Sophie and for the situation regarding all of them both at Lilyville and Swallowfield. Everything seemed so incredibly complicated, at present, and she could see no end to it. Martin respected her contemplative mood and did not intrude. Rejoining him she said, 'Thanks for bringing me here, Martin. I really appreciate it.'

As they left the church he slipped his arm about her waist.

'You must try not to worry too much about your aunt, Bethany. I'm sure she'll be all right.'

On the drive back to St. Helier he seemed rather preoccupied with the meeting he had to attend. To her relief, he did not attempt to do more than kiss her on the cheek as they left to go their separate ways. She knew that she had enjoyed the afternoon because there had been no demands on her emotions. She wondered if she was being unfair to Martin because, even though she found him very good company, she knew that she could never regard him as anything other than a friend.

She was making her way to the bus stop when she realised that she had promised to get some flowers for Sophie. It wasn't difficult to locate a florist's, but it did rather delay her and, by the time she returned to

Lilyville she found Amber and her father in the kitchen making a start on supper.

'It's all right,' Peter Tyler said. 'We're enjoying ourselves. We thought something simple tonight so we've raided the freezer and found some fish. Nicki's prepared a mountain of fresh vegetables . . . What's so funny?'

She told them about the enormous platter of fish and chips she had eaten for lunch. 'Never mind, I'll just have a salad . . . Now for dessert I've bought these.' And she produced a selection of fruit tarts that she had bought in a local patisserie, and some Jersey cream. 'I suppose we ought to have a starter — how about some soup?'

It was like old times — the three of them working together in the kitchen and Bethany realised that this was what had gone wrong lately. They had all become so involved in their own affairs that they had not really had time for each other.

Amber had spent the day with the Vautiers. 'James is heaps better and Mr. Vautier is going to take us out on 'The Seagull' just as soon as he's got her back from France. It's incredible that there was only minor damage, probably because she was located and brought in so quickly.'

'I still don't understand how those criminals

251

got ashore with all that jewellery. They mus
have been good swimmers,' Peter said.

'Oh, don't let's talk about it any more fo
now,' Bethany shuddered. 'Time enough fo
that when the trial comes up. I'm just so
thankful that Amber and James have suffered
no ill effects after their ordeal.'

Dinner was almost ready when Justin and
Fenella returned. Justin was busily mixing
cocktails when Amber and Bethany entered
the sitting-room.

'Dinner will be served in about fifteen
minutes milord,' Amber said with a little
curtsey.

Fenella took her drink from Justin. 'Oh, but
I'm afraid you must count us out — we've
been invited to some friends tonight.'

Justin frowned. 'Fenella, I thought you
had 'phoned to let Peter know we wouldn't
be here.'

'Did you darling? We must have got our
wires crossed. Never mind, I'm sure your
guests have got good appetites.'

Amber looked so disappointed that Bethany
felt a rush of anger towards Fenella, but tried
to hide her feelings. 'Oh well, not to worry
. . . How's Aunt Sophie? We're going to visit
her presently.'

'She's quite bright,' Justin informed her
'Really remarkable, in the circumstances.'

Fenella sipped her drink. 'Actually I thought she seemed rather tired. Perhaps you oughtn't to visit her tonight. She's going to need plenty of rest.'

'I'm sure she'll be pleased to see you for a little while,' Justin said. 'I'm sorry about dinner, Amber. Can you forgive me?'

'I'll try, but it might prove difficult. Are we still going riding in the morning?'

'But, of course. It's all arranged.' He looked across at Bethany. 'I hope you'll be able to join us this time, Beth.'

'Thanks, I'll look forward to it,' she told him, her heart hammering.

'Riding! But I thought we'd be having our usual early morning swim, J.C.' Fenella looked disconcerted.

Memories of that other swim crowded into Bethany's mind and she had a feeling that Fenella was goading her in some way. With a mumbled excuse about seeing to the dinner, she hurried out of the room with Amber close on her heels.

'That woman!' Amber exploded as soon as they reached the kitchen.

'What's wrong? Doesn't she like fish?' their father asked. They were just explaining what had happened when Justin put his head round the door.

'I'm so sorry that we're not able to sample

your meal. It's one of those unfortunate mix ups. Is it something we can have tomorrow?'

'Hardly,' Bethany said, refusing to meet his gaze. 'Never mind, I suppose there's always another occasion.'

'I'm afraid I'm not being much of a host going out and leaving my guests to fend for themselves. I do hope you don't mind, but it was really unavoidable.'

'It's no problem,' Peter assured him. 'You go off and enjoy yourselves.'

It was probably just as well, Bethany thought, for she found it difficult seeing Fenella and Justin together and realised that she was beginning to feel resentful towards the older woman who seemed to be doing everything in her power to be uncooperative.

Sophie, at least, was pleased to see them and perked up considerably. She lay back on the pillows looking pale, but better than Bethany had anticipated.

'Everyone is being so kind. Dr. Mauger popped in to see me this afternoon — such a busy man — and then dear Fenella and Justin came. I feel like royalty with so much attention.'

'Fenella and Justin have gone out to dinner,' Amber informed her.

'Yes, I know, dear. It's lovely to see them back together again. They make such a charming couple, don't you think?'

Bethany had to admit that they did. She concentrated on arranging the flowers that they had brought, although the room already looked like a florist's shop.

'Did they tell you that the operation was successful? Of course, I don't suppose I shall be told everything until my check-up, but it seems that the tumour was benign, thank God! No-one can imagine what a relief that is!'

'That is good news,' Peter said, patting her hand.

'Have you finished reading those diaries yet, Bethany?' Sophie wanted to know.

'Not quite — I'm finding them very interesting reading.'

They did not stay too long, for it was obvious that Sophie was far more tired than she was admitting.

'So you've been reading your grandmother's diaries. What do you make of them?' asked Peter on the way back to Lilyville.

'You should see them,' interrupted Amber. 'They're better than any romantic novel. This is the real thing — all about the love affair between Grandma and Cedric!'

'You've only looked at a couple of entries,

Amber! It's certainly been interesting filling in the gaps in our family history, but there are still several unanswered questions that I can't quite bring myself to ask Aunt Sophie.'

'Give me a for instance, Beth.'

'Well, it's as if Katherine loved both Grandpa and Cedric. I'm beginning to believe that's why she didn't push for a divorce . . . ' She paused. 'And then there was Cedric's son.'

'Go on,' her father was concentrating on his driving.

Bethany took a deep breath and voiced the thoughts she had been mulling over for the past few days. 'Well, I can't help wondering . . . Who exactly was Justin's grandmother? There's been no reference to her in all that I've read so far which seems strange . . . Was Cedric a widower when he met my grandmother?'

'Why don't you ask Justin?' put in Amber.

'Because we are delving into our family history and not his for the present,' her father told her. 'Perhaps you should finish reading the diaries and letters and then let me take a look, Beth. After all, there must surely be things I don't know too. And then we can compare notes.'

'Why bother?' Amber said impatiently.

'After all, it's not that important surely — not what happened in the dark ages.'

Peter Tyler laughed. 'It's delightful to know my two girls are so very different. Think of all the people that would be out of a job if we all thought that way.'

'I just don't see the point in dragging up the past — that's all.'

'But if we hadn't we wouldn't be here on this island at all, would we?' Bethany interjected.

'And you've enjoyed it, in spite of all the little hiccoughs, haven't you, Beth?' asked her father.

'Yes, of course.' If only because it had awakened her to what she had been missing out on in her life.

'I've had a wonderful time — so much so that I don't want to go home,' Amber informed them. 'James and I are going to keep in touch.'

'Well, what a surprise!' her father teased. 'It looks like there's going to be a mighty big 'phone bill.'

'Actually, we're going to write to each other. That's a thought — in years to come I wonder if someone will unearth our letters and want to know all about us . . . Perhaps I ought to keep a diary.'

'Well, that's a bit contradictory after what

you've been saying,' Bethany pointed out.

The conversation changed to their plans for the following day. The Vautiers were going out with friends and, on this occasion, Amber was not to be included. Bethany thought it was probably a good thing and that it would be pleasant to have a family day for a change.

Bethany found the early morning ride across the beach exhilerating, but suddenly she thought of Donovan and Mollie and longed to be back at Swallowfield. Looking at the expanse of golden sand stretching before her and the cobalt blue sea beyond, she knew that she would have found Jersey an idyllic place if only things could have been different between herself and Justin. Her whole body ached to be near him, but she was beginning to realise that it was a love that could never be reciprocated.

Justin looked wonderful on horseback. 'Are you enjoying the ride?' he asked, reigning in beside her.

'Yes, it's wonderful. Amber and the rest of the riders were ahead of them and, in a moment she knew they would have to catch up. There was so much that she wanted to say but, instead, she found herself telling him about her encounter with Lily the previous day.

'Leave it with me,' he said and urging his mount into a canter was off like the wind so that she had a job to keep pace with him. All too soon, however, the ride was over.

'That was ace!' declared Amber. 'A totally fantastic experience.'

'You seemed to be getting on very well with that boy in the checked jacket,' Justin commented.

She tossed back her blonde curls. 'Oh, he knew James — that's all. He was asking me about what happened last week-end.'

'I see.' Justin had a twinkle in his dark-brown eyes.

When they arrived back at Lilyville, Bethany went into the kitchen where she found Nicki looking distinctly upset.

'That Mrs. Moignard's just torn me off a strip for not fetching her breakfast, but yesterday she said she didn't want any. Now she's demanding grapefruit and muesli and we haven't got either.'

'Oh, I meant to pick up some muesli yesterday. I am sorry.'

'It's not just that — she's been at me for every little thing. Why aren't there any clean towels? Why is the coffee so strong? Why didn't I order her the right newspaper? I am trying to do my best, but it's hard with Mrs. Vibert being away.'

Bethany felt indignant on behalf of the young girl standing in front of her. She felt like marching up to Fenella and demanding to know why she was being so inconsiderate, but realised that it was not up to her to confront a house-guest of Justin's. Instead she said,

'Don't you worry, Nicki. You're doing just fine. Why don't you let me help you with some of the chores this morning?'

Together they prepared breakfast for the rest of the household. It appeared that Fenella had already left for St. Helier so that made matters easier for the time being. It suddenly dawned on Bethany that Fenella had been difficult because Justin had gone riding with them.

After breakfast she ignored Nicki's protests and vacuumed the upstairs landing, her own and her father's room and then instructed Amber to do hers.

'This isn't a hotel and we mustn't expect to be waited on hand and foot,' she told Amber, surveying her untidy room with disapproval.

Justin encountered her on the landing as she was dusting the oak table that stood in an alcove.

'This is ridiculous,' he said frowning. 'I don't expect my guests to do the cleaning.'

'Why not? We're not used to servants, apart from a domestic help who comes for a couple of hours a week — so be warned! We must all be more considerate towards Nicki — that's if you want to keep her. She's a good little worker, but rather sensitive and, at present, she does have five of us to think about with all our various needs.'

'Okay, I take your point, Beth. I'll have a word with her. Perhaps we ought to get someone else in for a few days.'

'Nonsense . . . I'm quite capable of helping out.'

He was blocking her way and, as she tried to get past, she caught her foot in the rug and would have lost her balance had he not been there to steady her. They ended up in a laughing heap in the doorway of her room and then, suddenly their eyes met in an intense gaze — pale grey with Vandyke brown.

Justin gently pulled her inside and pushed the door shut.

'What a fool I've been,' he murmured against her hair, 'to let Martin try and take you away from me.'

As his lips met hers she wanted to cry out, for the chemistry between them was so strong. She was swept away in an overwhelming rush of joy, for surely this meant he must care

261

for her, after all? His hands caressed her tenderly, filling her with exquisite sensations and sending all her resolutions to the wind. She smelt the fresh fragrance of him, felt his warm muscular body against hers . . . There was a sharp tap on the door and they sprang apart. It was Amber.

'Oh, sorry — was I interrupting something?' she asked innocently.

Bethany found it impossible to speak, but Justin said with ease,

'Not at all. We were just discussing what to have for dinner tonight, as a matter of fact . . . Can you be ready in about fifteen minutes? I've got an outing planned.'

When he had gone Amber turned to Bethany curiously.

'What's the matter, Beth? You looked so guilty when I came in.'

Bethany busied herself at the dressing table so that her sister could not see her expression. She was so hopelessly in love with Justin that she could not trust herself to be alone with him.

'There's nothing the matter, dear. We were just talking that's all.'

Amber's blue eyes widened. 'You were talking about James and me, weren't you?'

Bethany did not reply, relieved that Amber had jumped to this conclusion.

'I'm right, aren't I? Well, you've no need to worry. We are going for that sail on 'The Seagull', but, this time we'll be chaperoned by his grandparents.'

'That's just fine then. Now, we'd both better get ready for this outing.'

As she remembered Justin's kisses, a surge of love rose in her heart, but then cold reason hit her like a douche of cold water. What on earth was she thinking about? He was already involved with Fenella and probably just regarded her as an amusing diversion. She sighed, knowing that when she returned to Swallowfield everything would be put into perspective and Jersey would just seem like an enchanting dream.

11

Justin took them to Corbiere Point at the most Southwestern part of the island where the wild, rugged coastline had caused many a shipwreck. They got a good view of the famous lighthouse dominating the rocky headland.

Whilst Amber and her father went off to take some photographs, Justin and Bethany lingered behind enjoying the scenery.

'Amber seems to be having a good time,' Justin remarked. 'By the way, did you notice her chatting with that boy in the checked jacket on the ride this morning? I don't think you need worry about her becoming too involved with James Vautier. She's a pretty girl and naturally gregarious and I bet you that once she's back in England, the friendship between herself and James will cool off.'

'You think I'm being over protective, don't you?'

'No — of course not. It's natural that you're going to feel like that when you've been the mother figure in her life for the past few years. She'll be all right — she's proved that she's got a lot of commonsense and can take care of herself. You must consider yourself a bit more from now on.'

'Fat chance of that — someone's got to look after my family,' she snapped at him.

'I appreciate how hard it must be for you, but you've got your own life to lead too, just remember that.' He rested his hand lightly on her shoulder and it was as if an electric charge had been released. She wondered if he could have any idea of the extent of her feelings for him. However was she going to exist without him?

They had lunch at the Railway Carriage Coffee House which took them back to the era of the Jersey railway. As they sat enjoying the homemade fare, Bethany knew she should make the most of the time she spent with Justin and stop worrying about the future, but she found it difficult.

The four of them went to visit Sophie that afternoon. She was very cheerful and informed them that she was feeling a great deal better already.

'Dear Fenella popped in to see me at lunch-time in between her consultancy appointments. She brought me these magazines — wasn't that thoughtful?' She gave Justin a knowing look. 'Are you planning to take her out tonight?'

'Quite possibly. I haven't thought about it yet.'

The thought of Justin and Fenella having a quiet little candlelit dinner for two was more than Bethany could bear and she knew she was jealous. She suddenly felt thoroughly depressed.

They returned to Lilyville to find a message on the answer-phone from John Lawrence saying that he needed to speak urgently with Peter. He came out of the office looking rather harrassed and took Bethany on one side.

'This is difficult, Beth. John wants to have an extra couple of days off next week to prepare for his holiday. I can't very well say no, but I certainly can't expect Lily to run the place singlehanded, either. It simply wouldn't be fair on her, so it looks as if the options are to close the shop or return to England earlier than I'd anticipated.'

Bethany did some quick thinking. This could be the solution she was seeking. She suddenly made her mind up. It would be far better to make the break now before she made a complete fool of herself over Justin.

'Why you, Dad? Sophie seems to be out of the wood now and, when she's well enough to return here, Justin's talking of having a nurse in for a while, so why don't I go back to Sussex?'

Her father looked surprised to say the very least. 'But darling, I thought you were enjoying yourself here.'

'Oh, yes, I am,' she hastily assured him. 'But, you know me — I'm a bit of a homebird and so I'll be quite happy to return to Swallowfield.'

He gave her a shrewd look. 'There is something bothering you . . . It's not that dreadful Fenella getting to you, is it?'

She shook her head, wishing she could confide in him. Of course, he was right, for if it hadn't been for Fenella then the situation might have been very different. 'When would I need to be back?' she asked, resigning herself to this change of plan.

'Let me see now . . . I should think Tuesday at the very outside.'

'That soon!' Her thoughts were in a mad whirl. There were things she wanted to do — Lily's cousin to see for a final time, the diaries to finish reading and another painting to complete.

'Look why don't you sleep on it,' her father advised. 'You can always change your mind at the last minute, you know, and I'll go instead. In any case, I suppose we all ought to be returning soon, but it would be nice if I could finish cataloguing Sophie's books and then, of course, Amber would be so very disappointed . . . '

'It's all right, Dad, I'll go. It seems the easiest solution and I really don't mind — honestly.'

Her father gave her a hug. 'Thank you, darling. We always can depend on you.'

As Bethany sorted out something for supper that evening she thought of her return to Swallowfield and all the empty evenings that lay ahead. Justin had made her feel attractive and wanted again and, to a lesser degree, so had Martin. Anyway, at least she would have some good memories to treasure and no-one could take those away.

She realised that she would still have to cope with Justin's periodic appearances in Applebourne, but she would have some space to pull herself together and behave more rationally before then.

Presently, as she went into the hall, she encountered an irate Fenella having words with a tearful Nicki who ought to have gone home long since.

'Is there a problem?' Bethany enquired.

Fenella had gone white with anger. 'Well might you ask — this silly girl has managed to spoil one of my most expensive blouses by catching the iron on it. Well, I shall have to be recompensed. It will have to come out of her wages.'

'Did you ask Nicki to launder the blouse?' Bethany asked in a tight voice.

Fenella looked surprised. 'Yes, of course, and I also gave her strict instructions not to iron it.'

'No, Mrs. Moignard, you didn't say anything about that or I'd have remembered. I did my best — truly I did, but it's very difficult material and . . . '

'Might I suggest that if you don't like the way Nicki is doing your laundry that you attend to it yourself, as the rest of us do!' Bethany said in a frosty tone. 'Come along, Nicki. You've had a long, hard day and I'm going to make you a cup of tea!' And before Fenella could protest, Bethany had whisked the girl off into the kitchen.

A little later as Bethany was seeing to the evening meal, having pacified Nicki and packed her off home, Justin came into the kitchen.

'Before you say anything, I apologise if I've overstepped the mark.'

He poured himself some coffee from the bubbling percolator. 'I haven't the remotest idea of what you're talking about — unless it's got something to do with Fenella's blouse.'

269

'It really wasn't Nicki's fault. She did her best,' Bethany said defensively. To her irritation he began to laugh. 'I don't happen to think it's amusing!'

'Oh, but it is, believe you me! I only wish I'd been there to hear you telling Fenella to do her own laundry! . . . How's Nicki?'

'A bit overwrought, but a good night's sleep will no doubt put things right. She really can't be expected to pay for that blouse. She doesn't earn that sort of money!'

'You're a kind-hearted girl, Bethany Tyler. No-one need pay for it . . . Fenella could afford to buy twenty new blouses tomorrow if she wanted to, so don't give it another thought.' He brushed her cheek with a finger and she moved quickly away from him as if she had been stung.

'Are you planning to eat in tonight, after all?' she asked, trying to regain her composure.

'What? Oh, no — didn't I explain? Fenella and I are having something on the way to the airport. She's decided to return to Alderney tonight instead of tomorrow and she's been lucky enough to get a flight cancellation.'

'I didn't mean to upset your guest,' she said foolishly.

'Oh, Fenella will soon get over it. It's all a storm in a teacup. Anyway, she'll be back next week. She often comes to Jersey. It's the nature of her business. To her, flying between the islands is a bit like someone in England commuting to London so don't you worry.'

'Justin!' Fenella called imperiously and he paused in the doorway and gave Bethany one of his devastating smiles.

She forced herself to concentrate on cooking the supper and a moment or two later Fenella appeared.

'Ah, here you are, Bethany . . . Justin's probably told you that I've decided to leave tonight. If I were you, I wouldn't interfere in his domestic problems again. He won't say anything, but he doesn't like it. I realise that you come from a different sort of background and are not used to dealing with the domestics in the same way as the rest of us are. I've advised Justin to get rid of that silly little creature. The sooner Mrs. Vibert gets back and restores this house to order the better.'

Bethany, inwardly fuming at Fenella's remarks, nevertheless decided that it was better to ignore them and merely said sweetly,

'Well, it was nice to have met you, Fenella. I'm sure Sophie was pleased to see you.'

'Ah dear Sophie! I do so hope things will

be back to normal here before she returns. She certainly won't want to be bothered with this kind of trivia . . . Heavens is that the time? I mustn't keep J.C. waiting. Oh and just one more thing, darling. A piece of advice. Don't go eating your heart out for Justin because he's already spoken for!'

And she flounced out of the kitchen leaving Bethany staring after her in bewildered indignation. She felt the colour rise to her cheeks, as she realised that she must have been more transparent than she had imagined where her feelings for Justin were concerned. Perhaps he was so amused by her obvious infatuation with him that he had mentioned it to Fenella.

After supper, she collected the diaries from her room and, taking them into the summer house, curled up on one of the chairs to finish reading them. There were one or two things she needed to get straight in her mind.

It was late when she finally went to bed but, even then, she could not sleep. If she hadn't already decided to return to Swallowfield then she certainly would have done so by now. Why had Justin kept the truth from them? At two o'clock, she switched the light back on and picked up the last diary again, just to check that she hadn't made a mistake. The words jumped out of the page at her.

'The doctor confirmed today that I am pregnant. I could not be happier. Cedric and I love each other so very much . . . '

She flicked over the pages. The birth of a baby boy was recorded in the September of that year. It was apparently a difficult birth and the baby was delicate, but Katherine and Cedric were ecstatic and so was Sophie. This then was the child Marjorie Touzel had alluded to. They named him Justin John Cedric Rochel! The facts were indsputably there in black and white. Justin Rochel's grandmother was Katherine Tyler — her own grandmother, which would make Justin her cousin, and yet he had emphatically insisted that they were not related. Why would he do that when he had invited her to read the diaries and must, therefore, have some inkling of what they contained? And what of her father? Was he aware that Cedric's son had, in fact, been his half brother? On reflection, she was sure that she had heard Justin's father referred to as John, and so he had obviously been known by his second name.

The entries in the diary petered out shortly after Justin John's birth, but Bethany had learnt all she needed to know. She felt deeply hurt that Justin had deceived her and could not understand his motive in refusing to acknowledge that they shared the same grandmother. She wondered if she would have been prepared to have a relationship with him had she known the truth. She supposed there must be countless people who married their cousins and, after all, there was no law against it. In any case, they had different grandfathers. What on earth was she thinking of? They weren't having a relationship and Fenella had made it patently clear that she and Justin were more than friends.

Bethany drifted into an uneasy sleep and awoke when Nicki brought her in some early morning tea. The girl's pleasant face was all smiles.

'Oh Miss Tyler, I feel ever so much better this morning — and Mrs. Moignard has left.'

'I am glad Nicki — that you're feeling better, I mean,' she added hastily. 'And Mrs. Vibert will be back next Tuesday so it's not much longer to go now.'

The very day that she was returning to Applebourne, she reminded herself.

Nicki pulled back the curtains. 'I wasn't quite myself yesterday. I had a bit of a row with my boyfriend the night before and everything seemed twice as bad,' she confided.

'But you've obviously made it up?'

Nicki nodded, stars in her eyes. 'He proposed and I accepted! We're getting the ring on my afternoon off.'

'Congratulations!' It seemed that everybody's problems were being resolved except for her own.

When she went onto the terrace for breakfast, Justin was already there.

'Why didn't you tell me you're returning to Applebourne next Tuesday?' he demanded. Catching her by the arm he swung her round to face him.

'What's wrong, Beth?'

'I think you've been somewhat economical with the truth.'

'Would you mind explaining that statement?' His face was dangerously close to hers. She swallowed hard.

'Would you mind letting go of me?'

'I will just so soon as you've told me what's bothering you.'

'You are!' she informed him, meeting those wonderful dark eyes defiantly. She wanted to pour out everything to him — all her doubts, the things that were troubling her and to challenge him about his relationship with Fenella and demand to know how serious it was. Most of all, she wanted to melt into his arms and tell him that she loved him and that nothing else mattered — just so long as he cared for her. In the event, however, she did none of this because Amber, who had decided to help with breakfast, appeared just then carrying a laden tray.

Amber's questioning look spoke volumes and Bethany knew that now her sister would think she had found them both in a compromising situation.

A few moments later Peter Tyler came out onto the terrace looking serious. 'The hospital's just rung. Apparently, Sophie has had a bit of a relapse. Some medication hasn't agreed with her. They say not to worry as this sort of thing does happen, but one can't help being concerned all the same.'

They were rather a solemn party over breakfast, but it was impossible to repress Amber's high spirits for long. This week-end, everything boded well for her postponed sailing trip. The Vautiers had invited Amber to go with them to St. Malo in order to fetch 'The Seagull' back and she was over the moon.

'I thought I'd go into St. Helier this morning to the library,' Peter Tyler announced. 'And we'd better sort out your ticket for next

Tuesday too, Beth, if you're quite certain.'

She nodded and Amber said, 'What do you mean? Where are you going, Beth?'

'Someone has to relieve John Lawrence at the shop and so I've volunteered. Don't look like that, Amber. We knew we had to honour his holiday and anyway, there are things to sort out at Swallowfield.'

Even as Bethany said this she knew that it was herself who needed sorting out as much as anything else. She needed some space alone to get her thoughts together.

'I was all set to go,' her father said, 'but Beth simply wouldn't hear of it.'

'You always were a glutton for punishment.' Amber got up from the table. 'I suppose you realise you're going to be away for my birthday or had you forgotten?'

'Of course not,' Bethany said uncomfortably. 'I'll 'phone you.'

'It won't be the same . . . Well, if you'll excuse me folks, I've things to do — people to see.'

'Absolutely,' Justin replied. 'Just don't go getting locked in any more warehouses, will you? Our nerves won't stand the strain.'

'Okay,' she grinned. 'Give Aunt Sophie my love.'

As his younger daughter hurried away Peter Tyler said, 'Amber's had a marvellous time, Justin. We all have.'

'In spite of all the problems?'

'Oh, they've added another dimension.'

'And do you think we'll manage to live in such harmony at Swallowfield?'

Justin was looking directly at Bethany as he asked this, and she averted her gaze, busying herself by collecting the plates together.

'I don't see why not,' her father said. 'We're all pretty congenial people so we should be able to rub along together, shouldn't we?'

'What do you think, Bethany?' Justin asked putting her on the spot.

'We'll just have to wait and see how things work out, won't we?' she murmured.

'Yes, I suppose we will . . . What are you planning to do this morning?'

'Actually I was hoping to get to see Marjorie Touzel for one last time.'

'Excellent — I'll take you over there in around an hour.' She was flummoxed, not wanting to be alone with him at present and he saw her hesitation. 'No buts, I insist — I'll see you presently.'

Upstairs Amber was busily stuffing additional clothes into a hold-all.

'I want to be prepared for all eventualities. After all, we might go to a French restaurant tonight or even stay in a hotel.'

'We'll need to pay our share,' Bethany said worriedly. 'Have you spoken to Daddy about money?'

'Yes, of course, and he's going to have a word with Rupert Vautier . . . Beth, what's up between you and Justin? And don't say nothing! It was obvious you'd been having words when I came out with the breakfast this morning.'

So that was what she thought! 'You've got it all wrong, darling. I was a bit worried about one or two things, that's all, and Justin was putting my mind at rest.'

'Amber!' their father called before anything further could be said. 'The Vautiers are here.' Amber snatched up her bag and was out of the room in a flash, a hurried 'Goodbye' thrown over her shoulder.

Collecting her paints, Bethany went downstairs and settled herself on the terrace to finish her flower painting — another lily. She hoped there might be time to do just one more before leaving the island.

Justin found her there, engrossed in what she was doing. He peered over her shoulder. 'That's beautiful . . . I know Paul is hoping you'll keep him supplied with your paintings when you get back to England. He's got plenty of ideas in mind for running off some prints for birthday cards etc. Of course, if you go in for this in a big way, you'll need to employ me as your accountant.'

'But perhaps I don't want to turn my hobby into a business enterprise. Anyway, this painting isn't for sale.'

'Oh,' he sounded disappointed. He was standing so close to her that she caught her breath.

'What is it then — a souvenir of your holiday?'

'No, it's a present for Sophie. I thought she might like it.'

'That's a sweet thought. I'm sure she will.' He kissed the top of her head.

'I think you should stop flirting with me,' she said, her pulse racing uncontrollably.

'Oh, you do, do you? To what do I owe this sudden change of heart?'

'Think about it,' she advised him. 'We're going to be seeing more of each other in Sussex and so, before you come to Applebourne, I think we should get a few things straightened out.'

'Go on — I'm listening.'

'Oh, why are you making this so very difficult for me?'

'We had an unfinished conversation earlier this morning so perhaps we ought to get it finished now before there are any more interruptions. Why don't you tell me just what's been going on in that pretty head of yours?'

'As if you didn't know ... What about Fenella?'

'What about her?' He looked mystified.

'You know very well what I'm trying to say,' she told him crossly.

'If I did, I'd hardly be asking you — you seem to be talking in riddles.'

'Then I'll be more direct. Are you planning to get married?'

'What an interesting thought ... ' There was an amused looked in his dark eyes. 'And, if I am, would that bother you?'

'Yes, no — oh, I don't know ... Now here comes Dad!'

Peter Tyler, totally unaware of his daughter's consternation, strolled onto the terrace, admired the painting and said, 'Justin, I thought I might look in at the antique shop this afternoon after visiting Sophie. Are there any messages?'

They wandered into the house together deep in conversation, leaving Bethany to pack away her paints. Suddenly she longed to be back in Applebourne and see Mags so that she could share with her all that had gone on during her stay at Lilyville. Was it possible that so much could have happened in such a short space of time? It seemed like a lifetime since they had left Swallowfield.

She was ready and waiting when Justin reappeared dangling the car keys. 'Right, I've put everything on hold until late afternoon. There are a few things we need to get sorted out before you return to England and one concerns Marjorie Touzel.'

'There must be something we can do for her.'

He shook his head. 'At the end of the day it could be said that it's none of our business. After all, there are no signs of neglect and she is well looked after.'

'But she's not happy,' persisted Bethany, 'and that's important when you're growing old, isn't it? Couldn't you have a word with her son — find out what's been going on to upset his mother.'

'I'll certainly see what I can do,' he promised. 'You're a kind-hearted girl, Bethany Tyler.'

In the event, everything worked out far better than they could possibly have anticipated. Edward Touzel was off sick from work when they arrived and his wife was out shopping. Whilst Bethany had a cup of tea with Marjorie, Justin went into the garden with her son on the pretext of looking at the new greenhouse. What transpired between them Bethany could only guess at, but she felt sure that Justin would have some influence with the younger man. Presently they returned to the sitting room looking rather sombre.

'Mum, whyever didn't you tell me you wanted to go to see Lily?'

'I thought you wouldn't like it. Anyway, I don't have the money.'

Edward Touzel had the grace to look shame-faced. 'We didn't want to worry you with money matters. We'll sit down and discuss it all presently.'

'You know I'd have let you have whatever you wanted, if only you'd asked me, Ed, but it's the deceit I couldn't stand. I trusted you to look after my money — thought you knew what you were doing. I just wanted enough to have a holiday with Lily and treat myself occasionally . . . You haven't got through it all, lad, have you?'

Edward sank down on the settee and ran his fingers through his shock of sandy hair. 'I admit I've borrowed some of your money without asking you, but I'll pay it back, I promise you, every penny. I'm afraid I've been rather foolish and run up a few debts.'

'I suspected as much,' Marjorie Touzel said. 'Well, thank goodness it's all out in the open at last.'

'Mr. Rochel's going to help me sort things

out . . . He's an accountant, you know.'

Justin moved towards the door. 'We'll leave these good people to have a talk, Bethany.'

'When shall I tell Lily to expect you?' Bethany asked Marjorie.

Edward Touzel shook her hand. 'We'll both come, Miss Tyler, just so soon as i can be arranged and then, when we get back we'll make a fresh start.'

A few minutes later, as they drove away Bethany turned to Justin.

'Do you think he really meant what he said?'

'Oh, he meant it, all right. You see he's found out his wife's been carrying on with another man and that's why she's been running up so many debts. It's Rita Touzel he's been bailing out all this time All the money he's spent has been for her benefit — or so he thought — and now he's discovered she's been laundering his account. That's why he's off sick today because he just can't face going in. He's a weak man and deep down, he's really fond of his mother.'

'So what's going to happen now?'

'Well, hopefully, he's come to his senses in so far as his extravagant wife is concerned but that side of things he'll have to sort ou for himself. In actual fact, we're not talking about a large sum of money — just a relatively small nestegg by today's standards and so I have every confidence that eventually Edward Touzel will manage to pay his mother back. For a start he's going to sell the new car his wife persuaded him to buy. He's got a rather poorly paid job, but he does have the chance of overtime.'

'I suppose that now he's aware of what's been going on he can put a stop to it. Poor Mrs. Touzel.'

'Yes, I have promised to help them and I'll certainly do all I can. But it's not all bad,' he assured her. 'Marjorie Touzel has been reluctant to spend money on repairs over the years and, during the short while that Edward and his wife have been there, they've had quite a lot of improvements done to the place and he assures me they were paid for out of his earnings. If his wife decides to stay with him then I reckon things will be very different in that household from now on.'

'What a mess some people seem to make of their lives,' Bethany mused.

'Well, it's a good job you took an interest in the old lady's welfare, isn't it? I think it'll work out all right for her — even if not for her son . . . And now that we've

sorted out their problems, I think we've
got some sorting out of our own to do
don't you?'

'Yes,' she agreed, her heart pounding
wildly, 'just a bit.'

12

Justin took Bethany to Retreat Farm in St. Lawrence where they had lunch in the Café des Fleurs before looking round.

'It's a working nursery and the world's largest mail order florist — larger than Wembley Stadium in fact,' he informed her.

As they sat in the pleasant atmosphere of the café enjoying a salad platter, he said, 'So come on, what's on your mind? It's taken me rather a long time to find some space for us to discuss things.'

Bethany took a deep breath, 'I still don't understand why you want to own part of Swallowfield when you're obviously thinking of getting married.'

Justin had a long sip of the cool drink in front of him. 'I think it might be the ideal place to bring a new bride.'

So he wasn't going to deny it. 'But why, when you've got Lilyville?'

He sighed. 'We've already been through this at least a dozen and one times, Bethany. I need a base for when I'm in England and Applebourne is near enough to London to make it a good centre for me. I like the peace and quiet of village life and I like Swallowfield. What more can I say to convince you?'

'And your wife?' she persisted, determined to get things straight.

'Oh, I've no doubt she'll like it too. Yes, it'll suit us both very well once we've made a few necessary alterations.'

Suddenly she lost her appetite. It had been a good morning, but thoughts of Fenella kept crowding in.

He gave her a keen look from those dark brown eyes. 'You're still not happy with the idea. Why not, may I ask?'

'I just keep wondering how we'll all get on under one roof, if you must know.'

'Oh, I think we'll manage fine — just you wait and see. Now what else is there?'

'As I told you this morning, I think you've been somewhat economical with the truth.'

'Good gracious girl, what are you accusing me of now!' he said so loudly that the elderly couple seated at the next table gave them a strange look. Bethany coloured painfully and he put a hand over hers and lowered his voice. 'Sorry, but I can't put things right if I don't know what the problem is, can I?'

'Oh, but you do. You know I've been reading the diaries. After all, it was you who suggested it in the first place.'

He rubbed his chin. 'Yes, because I thought it would help you to understand some of the background to your grandparents' separation, amongst other things.'

'Then you must know what's in them and, surely you would expect me to be more than a little confused that you've told me we're not related when, in fact, according to the diaries, we are!'

He shook his head vehemently. 'No, Bethany, we're not — not at all. I honestly don't know where you're coming from on this one.'

Bewildered, her head in a whirl, she said, 'But, in the diaries my grandmother wrote that she had a baby by Cedric — a boy called Justin John.'

There was an incredulous expression on his face. 'Surely you don't think that Katherine was my grandmother . . . '

As she stared at him uncertainly, he began to laugh.

'I don't see what's so funny,' she told him crossly.

'Then let me enlighten you . . . Have you got any idea of how old I am?'

'In your thirties, I suppose, but what on earth has that got to do with anything?'

'I'm thirty five, Beth. Justin John would

have been younger than Sophie had he survived, but, unfortunately, he died in infancy. So, don't you see, it would have been impossible for him to have been my father on two counts. You obviously haven't read all the diaries, have you?'

She shook her head. 'I thought I had, but the third one petered out shortly after the baby was born.'

'Perhaps Sophie thought there would be questions and wanted you to discuss things with her before giving you the others.' he said gently.

'So if Katherine wasn't your grandmother then — who was?'

'Cedric's family came from Guernsey. He had a brother, William, whose wife had died in childbirth. The child had survived — a boy called John. When William had the chance of working abroad, Cedric and Katherine offered to take care of John who was about nine or ten by then, I suppose.'

Light suddenly dawned. 'And John was your father?'

Justin nodded. 'As the years went by William remarried and settled in America. By then John was old enough to make his own decisions and he chose to stay at Lilyville with Cedric and Katherine whom he had come to regard as his parents. And so, you see, Cedric Rochel was not really my grandfather at all, but my great uncle. Now do you understand?'

'Yes, I think so. You must think me very foolish, Justin and, if I've hurt you by prying into the past then I'm sorry.'

'You haven't, I can assure you of that. I had a wonderful secure upbringing and then, when I was fourteen, my parents died and I was taken into the warmest family you could ever imagine. Cedric and Katherine may not have been my real grandparents, but they were certainly the only ones that I needed. So you see we really aren't related at all. I had no intention of deceiving you, I can assure you. It's just been an unfortunate misunderstanding. And now that we've got all that out in the open shall we take a look around this place?'

She followed him out into the sunshine, wondering however she could have been so foolish as to have doubted him in the first place.

The spectacle of seven acres of carnations growing under glass was breathtaking. As they walked round, Bethany was amazed to learn that these lovely flowers could be dated back to the Ancient Greeks or perhaps even earlier.

'Thought you'd like it,' Justin said, a

satisfied expression on his face. 'You see, in spite of our differences, I do know you well enough to tell what will please you. Let's get some carnations delivered to Sophie, shall we?'

Afterwards, they went to look at the exotic parrot aviaries and, just for a short while, she forgot her problems. They could have been on a tropical island and she imagined what it would be like to be completely alone with him. She sighed and he shot her a glance.

'What's wrong, Beth? That was heartfelt. Are you thinking of going home, perhaps?'

She nodded. 'It's always difficult to return to the real world after a holiday, isn't it?'

'Just remember one thing, Beth . . . '

She turned to look at him questioningly. 'I'm here for you should you need me . . . I don't want you to think that you have to cope on your own ever again.'

The thought filled her with a tiny surge of hope, but then she remembered Fenella and it died away again.

After a brief visit to Sophie who was still feeling rather unwell, they returned to Lilyville and Justin produced the two missing diaries. Bethany was still reading them when her father arrived back some time later.

'I popped into the hospital, but Sophie

was fast asleep so I only stayed for a few minutes.'

Bethany got to her feet. 'Would you like some tea?'

'That would be nice — and then, darling, I'd like to talk.'

When she returned, a short while later, he had picked up one of the diaries and was thumbing through it. Over tea they discussed the revelations made by Katherine in her journals. Peter Tyler told Bethany that he and Sophie had only recently had a heart to heart about family matters.

'So are you happier about things now?' he asked.

'I suppose so except . . . ' She hesitated. 'I still can't make out why my own grandfather was so uncaring where Sophie was concerned.'

'Can't you? Then you obviously haven't read my mother's letters.'

There was a wealth of meaning in her father's voice. Bethany looked at him, her eyes widening. 'Surely you can't mean . . . ?'

'Your grandfather adored my mother and was insanely jealous when, early on in the marriage, she came here to visit her parents and, on her return to Swallowfield, mentioned the lodger — Cedric Rochel. Your grandfather believed that Sophie was Cedric's daughter. You see, unfortunately, she was born a few weeks premature which fitted in with the time that summer when my mother had stayed here!'

'And was she?' Bethany found herself asking.

He shook his head. 'No — my mother was undoubtedly attracted to Cedric from the time they first met and flattered by his attention, but she once told Sophie that she was always faithful to my father and that she did not begin a proper relationship with Cedric until well after she left him, and there is absolutely no reason to doubt that!'

Bethany sipped her tea. 'It's a sad story and I suppose none of it would have happened if my grandfather had been more trusting. I loved him dearly, but I suppose he could be rather stubborn.'

Her father laughed. 'That's putting it mildly and I'm a chip off the old block, aren't I? Darling, I know you haven't really accepted my decision to agree to Sophie selling her share in Swallowfield to Justin.'

'Oh, I've come to terms with it now, although I have to say that Sophie seems fairly well cushioned here and Justin is obviously not going to throw her out on the street, even if he might feel she needs to economise on the entertaining!'

Peter gave an odd little smile. 'The thing is, Beth you still haven't got the whole picture . . . '

'Whatever do you mean?' What further revelations could there possibly be now? Her father poured himself more tea as if to fortify himself.

'As you are aware, I made some very unwise investments some years ago on the advice of someone I considered to be a friend.' Bethany nodded. 'As a result, shortly after your grandmother died, I was faced with mortgaging the house to prevent us and the business from going under.'

She stared at him aghast; she had known things were bad, but not that bad. 'Why on earth didn't you see fit to tell me all this before?'

'At the time you were still at university. I didn't want to worry your mother and, quite frankly, I was at my wits end. Also I couldn't, in all fairness, do anything without consulting Sophie. After all, by then half the house belonged to her. Sophie was remarkably understanding in the circumstances. I came over here for a few days, ostensibly to look at some books she wanted to sell but, in reality, to see if we could find a way out of the mess I was in. I already had a bank loan for the business and was finding it enough of a struggle to pay that back and I'd sold just about everything else I could think o to keep us afloat.'

'So what happened?' Bethany prompted him gently.

'I believed, at the time, that Sophie must have inherited money from our mother although now, of course, I know differently It wasn't until recently when Justin told me that I realised what a sacrifice Sophie had made on my behalf. Unbeknown to me, she had very little capital available, but she did have some valuable antique jewellery and silverware and so she sold most of that to provide me with an interest free loan to prevent me from taking out a mortgage. So you see I owe such a lot to Sophie. We have a roof over our heads and the business is still thriving. All right we're not making a fortune but we are keeping our heads above water and I've managed to pay off the bank loan.'

'Oh, Dad, whyever couldn't you have told me all this at the outset?'

'You've had quite enough to cope with these past years, Beth. Anyway, I've tried desperately hard to pay off some of Sophie's loan and to give her a small share of the profits from the bookshop, but then during the recession, it became impossible even to do that and now she really needs her capital

I'm afraid I've reached the conclusion that I'm just not a very good business man, darling.'

She put her arm about his shoulder. 'That doesn't matter to me because you're the best father anyone could wish to have.'

'But I seem to have failed you and Amber in a number of ways recently,' he said wearily.

She hugged him. 'It was hardly your fault that you were made redundant from your city job or that you were given bad financial advice. Anyway, we much prefer you working at the bookshop, even if it has produced so much hassle of late. I'm glad we've been able to have this holiday together. It's what we all needed and it's helped put things in perspective and drawn us closer together as a family.'

He nodded. 'You're right. We were drifting, weren't we? All going our own separate ways.'

'Yes, I think we were.' She was unsure of how it had happened, but it was as if they had all been so involved in their own problems that they had not seemed to be aware of each other's needs. She collected up the tea-things.

'I'm glad you've told me everything at last. Let's not keep any more secrets from each other in future. Now I'm going to ring Martin Mauger. I'd like to see him again before I leave on Tuesday.'

She saw her father's expression and realised what he must be thinking. 'It was just a holiday friendship, Dad, nothing serious, but I do like him and if he's ever in England I hope he'll look us up.'

Her father laughed. 'You mean you hope he'll look you up! Well I'm glad to see you're beginning to pick up your life again, Beth. You've had a rough time these past few years.'

Martin was disappointed to learn that Bethany was returning to England so soon and arranged to take her out to dinner the following evening.

After church on Sunday morning, Bethany sat in the garden trying to complete another painting, but her mind was elsewhere. She found herself thinking of Applebourne and all her friends there and knew that that was where she most wanted to be right now. She had recharged her batteries, had the opportunity to sort things out with her family and she realised that the bond between her father, Amber and herself was now stronger than ever, and that they would all be more aware of each other's needs from now on.

As for Justin, how could she have been so

foolish as to have believed that he cared for her, when he had obviously just been using her in order to make Fenella jealous? She wondered what her father would say if he knew how she had behaved this holiday? There must have been something intoxicating in the air! She was normally such a sensible person and would just have to learn to control her feelings when Justin came to Swallowfield, however hard it might prove to be.

That afternoon, Justin had arranged to take Peter to visit an elderly gentleman who had been a friend of Cedric Rochel's and had an impressive private collection of books and antiques. First they dropped Bethany off at the hospital.

Sophie looked rather pale and tired, but perked up when she saw Bethany. She indicated the carnations.

'What a lovely surprise! I don't deserve all this attention, but I have to say I enjoy it. Thank you so much. Where are Justin and Peter?'

Bethany explained saying that they would be calling in later.

'Peter tells me you're leaving us on Tuesday to go back to Applebourne.'

'Yes, I'm needed at the shop. You won't mind, will you Aunt Sophie? You're much better now, aren't you?'

Her aunt took her hands. 'Indeed I am dear, and you've all played a part. It's done me a power of good knowing that our families are reunited again after all this time. I've loved having you around, and I'm only sorry that you've had to come at a time when I've not been the best of hostesses.'

Bethany bent and kissed her aunt. 'Surely in families there's no need to stand on ceremony? It doesn't matter if we know each other warts and all.'

Aunt Sophie laughed. 'That's one way of putting it, I suppose.'

'I've finished reading all the diaries and Justin, my father and myself, have had a bit of a heart to heart about things.'

'And did you reach any conclusions?' Her aunt's grey eyes never strayed from Bethany's face.

'Only that it's good that things are out in the open so that now we can put the past to rest once and for all and bury all our differences along with it.'

She nodded. 'I'm glad you've seen it that way. You have no idea how pleased I am that there are no longer any bad feelings between us. I just want everyone to get on and to be happy.'

That could prove to be a bit of a tall order,

Bethany reflected, because the one thing that could make her happy was well and truly out of her reach and there was nothing anyone could do about that.

On her return to Lilyville, she managed to finish the painting before getting ready for her date with Martin. She dressed with care in an apple green two piece, brushing her hair until it shone and securing it with a velvet scrunchie borrowed from Amber. She put on rather more make-up than usual and was pleased with the result.

'Well,' Justin said, encountering her on the stairs. 'You must have known that I was planning to take you out for dinner tonight.'

She caught her breath. This couldn't be happening — not for a second time! 'I'm sorry, Justin, but how could I have known? I'm going out with Martin Mauger.'

His expression was impassive. 'Are you indeed! Then it's just as well that I haven't booked a table, isn't it? How presumptuous of me to suppose that you would wish to spend the evening with me.'

She swallowed hard. 'That's unfair, Justin, and you know it!'

But he had reached his landing and did not turn back. She bit her lip, feeling a dull ache in her throat. It could be the last time that she would have to spend any time with Justin before returning to England and now she had thrown even that opportunity away.

Her father came into the hall. 'You're looking very glam, darling. By the way, Justin was looking for you.'

'We met on the stairs,' she told him dully.

'Oh, good. I did tell you I'm out tonight, didn't I? Going to have a meal with a couple of Sophie's friends.'

She nodded, too miserable to speak. She realised that it wasn't very kind of her to go out with Martin when she was feeling like this.

In the event, however, she enjoyed herself. Martin took her to a French-style bistro where they sampled bouillabaisse, an interesting Provencal fish dish, followed by crepes for dessert. All this was washed down with a good wine and they finished off with liqueur coffees. Afterwards they went for a stroll.

'There's something I have to tell you,' Martin said. She thought he had been rather quiet during the meal and wondered what it was he was about to say. He slipped his arm casually through hers.

'I don't quite know how to tell you this. I didn't think it would happen and now it has.'

She waited with baited breath, not knowing what to expect.

'A few weeks ago I went for an interview for a job in America. I hadn't heard anything and assumed I hadn't been successful but then, out of the blue, last week I got a phone call and was offered the post. The contract is for a year in the first instance.'

She hugged him. 'Martin, that's wonderful news. You have accepted, haven't you?'

'I've got to let them know definitely by tomorrow. I wasn't sure what to do, Bethany. You see I really do care for you and I thought perhaps we had something special going for us.'

There might well have been, she reflected — if it hadn't been for Justin.

'I really have enjoyed your company, Martin,' She told him gently. 'You've helped to make this a memorable holiday and we can still write to each other if you like.'

He looked crestfallen. 'But what you're saying is that there is no prospect of it becoming more than a friendship?'

She knew she would have to let him down gently. 'Not at the moment, Martin, no, but, after all, we haven't known each other for very long, have we?'

He drove her back to Lilyville shortly after that and saw her to the front door.

He declined to come in for a coffee, but suddenly caught her in a tight embrace, giving her a long, tender kiss.

It was not until she had finished waving to him as he drove away that she realised Justin was standing in the doorway.

'Good evening, was it?' he asked and did not wait for her reply. She knew that this time he must have seen them kissing and that he had completely misconstrued the situation. That night her pillow was wet with bitter tears.

The following morning Amber returned full of her sailing trip. She was in irrepressible high spirits and her mood seemed to rub off on everyone else.

Justin was coldly polite towards Bethany and after a while Amber said, 'What's up with you two? Has something been going on that I don't know about?'

'I can't imagine what you're talking about, young lady!' Justin ruffled her hair and then they had a mad few minutes chasing round the garden whilst Bethany could only watch. Her father put a hand on her shoulder.

'She's right, isn't she, Beth? Was it because you went out with Martin yesterday evening.'

'Yes, I suppose so. If only I'd known Justin was planning to take me out to dinner.'

'He likes surprises, but it's not like him to

get so miffed . . . Is there something going on between you and Martin, darling?'

'No, I've told you. I think Martin might like there to be but . . . '

'You don't care for him in that way,eh?'

She shook her head. 'Anyway, he's going to America next month for a year.'

'I see. So why don't you tell Justin he's got it all wrong?'

'He — he saw Martin kissing me goodbye,' she said miserably.

Her father took her hands between his. 'You're in love with Justin, aren't you, darling?'

She was startled. 'I didn't know I was that transparent.'

'I'd be a strange father if I didn't, at least, attempt to know what was happening in my daughter's lives, wouldn't I? Perhaps you should make your feelings known to him.'

'What difference would that make? He's as good as told me he's going to marry Fenella and so I've just got to get used to the idea.'

Her father frowned. 'Are you sure about that? He hasn't said anything to me. I can't say I care over much for that young woman.'

'Then why don't you ask him? He's already indicated how much his wife will love Swallowfield.'

'Oh, darling — what can I say?'

For answer she gave him a hug, blinking away the tears.

Over lunch Justin announced, 'I thought before we visited Sophie this afternoon we'd take Beth on one last trip.'

Her heart soared. He had obviously got over being out of sorts with her.

'Where?' demanded Amber eagerly. 'Or can I choose?'

'Not this time, young lady,' her father intervened unexpectedly.

'It's somewhere I particularly wanted to take Beth before she returns to England,' Justin added.

It was only a short drive to St. Ouen and to Bethany's surprise, he pulled up outside The Gold Centre.

Amber was enthralled. 'This is different,' she breathed as they watched the goldsmiths at work.

Although the craftsmen took on commissions The Gold Centre also had a good range of designer jewellery.

'Did you know that gold has been used by craftsmen for over 6,000 years?' Justin informed them as they wandered round admiring the vast collection of jewellery. After a while, Bethany found herself on her own with him.

'If you were going to buy something special for a friend, what would you choose?' he asked.

She realised he must surely want her to help him select something for Fenella. 'If it were a female friend then I'd probably opt for a pair of earrings,' she said, a lump rising in her throat.

'Hmn — actually I was thinking of something rather larger — a necklace say.'

He had given himself away. It had to be a gift for Fenella. He pointed to a chunky necklace. 'What do you think of that?'

She tried to envisage Fenella wearing it. 'Ye-es, I suppose if your friend likes that kind of thing.'

'Come on, be honest, what do you like yourself?'

'Me? Oh, I'd have something simple like that little pendant over there.' She caught sight of the price tag and her eyes widened. 'That's rather deceptive.'

He smiled. 'You've got good taste. It's beautiful and just what I had in mind. Now I'm going to see what Amber would like for a birthday present.'

Bethany wandered off and met up with her father so she didn't know whether Justin actually purchased the pendant or not. They decided to buy Amber a watch for her birthday, from the pair of them.

Sophie was tearful when Bethany called to say goodbye.

'You will come and see me again, won't you my dear? I know England isn't that far away, but it seems like the other end of the earth at this moment.'

Bethany assured her that she would be back for another visit soon. Sophie took her hand. 'You and I are very alike in many ways, you know. I'm so very glad you came.'

★ ★ ★

During the short flight back to England, Bethany found memories of the past few weeks flooding in. She had been bitterly disappointed that morning when Justin had said his goodbyes over breakfast, for she had thought he would be driving her to the airport, but he had told her that he had some urgent business to attend to which would keep him occupied for the entire day.

When she reached Gatwick she suddenly realised that she had never felt so alone in her life. It was a straightforward train journey from there to Horsham, but she decided for once to splash out and get a taxi all the way to Applebourne. Swallowfield would seem so empty but, at least, it would give her a chance to sort herself out and she could always give Mags a ring and catch up on the latest village news.

The taxi driver carried her case to the front door. She inserted her key and stepped into the hall, but then her heart almost missed a beat for there were noises coming from the direction of the sitting-room. Her hand had already reached for the 'phone when Justin appeared in the doorway.

'Hallo, did you have a good journey?'

She stared at him, unable to believe her eyes and then, as that dear face broke into smiles and his arms outstretched in welcome, she ran to him and he swept her up, showering her with kisses.

'How could you ever have thought I'd have let you go off like that?' he murmured against her hair.

'But — how did you get here?' she asked in bewilderment.

'I caught an earlier flight, of course. Aren't you pleased to see me?'

For an answer she buried her face against his chest. 'Heh, that's a fine way to greet me!' he said stroking her hair.

'I'm so sorry about Saturday night,' she murmured.

'Oh that — your father explained about

Martin's job in America and I can quite see that you would want to wish him all the best, but did you have to look as if you were enjoying his kiss quite so much?'

Before she could reply he added, 'Anyway, apparently I'm not the only one to have got the wrong impression about things.'

He took her by the hand and led her into the sitting-room where she stood transfixed by the sight of a quantity of colourful carnations glowing like so many jewels.

'Flown in from Jersey today,' he said and then indicated a small box on the coffee table. 'Open it,' he commanded.

Wonderingly she did so. Inside was the pendant she had so carefully selected the previous day.

'But I don't understand,' she said.

He was studying her face. 'You do like it, don't you?'

'Of course.' She turned to him more bewildered than ever. 'But I thought it was for Fenella — unless . . . Is she coming here?'

'No Bethany,' he said gently. 'Fenella isn't coming here. The flowers and the necklace are for you.'

Brushing aside her hair, he fastened the pendant about her neck.

'It's beautiful. I don't know what to say,'

she told him, her pulse racing. There was something she still needed to get clear in her mind and she said in a rush, 'Justin are you — are you going to marry Fenella?'

He smiled that captivating, boyish smile of his. 'Whatever put that notion into your head? I've known Fenella for a long time and once, a few years back, we were briefly engaged, but it would never have worked because what we both want out of life is so very different. She is so materialistic and such a social butterfly . . . but I do know who I want for my wife.'

'Do you?' she asked wonderingly, her grey eyes meeting his dark ones.

'That's if you'll have me, of course.' He caught her in his arms. 'My dearest, darling Beth, will you marry me?'

A surge of happiness flooded her entire being. 'Yes, Justin — oh yes, because I love you with all my heart.'

His lips met hers then and they were transported to an island paradise of their own where the air was filled with the sweet perfume of flowers.

THE GREENWAY
Jane Adams

When Cassie and her twelve-year-old cousin Suzie had taken a short cut through an ancient Norfolk pathway, Suzie had simply vanished . . . Twenty years on, Cassie is still tormented by nightmares. She returns to Norfolk, determined to solve the mystery.

FORTY YEARS
ON THE WILD FRONTIER
Carl Breihan & W. Montgomery

Noted Western historian Carl Breihan has culled from the handwritten diaries of John Montgomery, grandfather of co-author Wayne Montgomery, new facts about Wyatt Earp, Doc Holliday, Bat Masterson and other famous and infamous men and women who gained notoriety when the Western Frontier was opened up.

TAKE NOW, PAY LATER
Joanna Dessau

This fiction based on fact is the love-turning-to-hate story of Robert Carr, Earl of Somerset, and his wife, Frances.